LEARNING CURVE

Visit us at www.boldstrokesbooks.com

What Reviewers Say About BOLD STROKES Authors

KIM BALDWIN

"*Force of Nature* is filled with nonstop, fast paced action. Tornadoes, raging fire blazes, heroic and daring rescues…Baldwin does a fine job of describing the fast-paced scenes and inspiring the reader to keep on turning the pages." – L-word.com Literature

ROSE BEECHAM

"…her characters seem fully capable of walking away from the particulars of whodunit and engaging the reader in other aspects of their lives." – *Lambda Book Report*

GEORGIA BEERS

"Beers weaves a tale of yearning, love, lust, and conflict resolution. She has constructed a believable plot, with strong characters in a charming setting." – *JustAboutWrite*

RONICA BLACK

"*Wild Abandon* tells how these two women come to realize that 'life was too precious to be ruled by…fears, by…demons.' While these two women struggle with their issues, there is some very, very hot sex. If you enjoy complex characters and passionate sex scenes, you'll love *Wild Abandon*." – *MegaScene*

GUN BROOKE

"*Course of Action* is a romance…populated with a host of captivating and amiable characters. The glimpses into the lifestyles of the rich and beautiful people are rather like guilty pleasures…a most satisfying and entertaining reading experience." – *Midwest Book Review*

CATE CULPEPPER

"…an exceptional storyteller who has taken on a very difficult subject …and turned it into a spellbinding novel. As an author, she understands well that fiction can teach us our own history." – *JustAboutWrite*

JANE FLETCHER

"*The Exile and the Sorcerer* is a mesmerizing read, a tour-de-force packed with adventure, ordeals, complex twists and turns, and the internal introspection of appealing characters." – *Midwest Book Review*

JD Glass

"*Punk Like Me*…is different. It is engaging. It is life-affirming. Frankly, it is genius. This is a rare book in that it has a soul; one that is laid bare for all to see." – *JustAboutWrite*

Grace Lennox

"*Chance* is refreshing…Every nuance is powerful and succinct. *Chance* is not a novel about the music industry; it is about a woman discovering herself as she muddles through all the trappings of fame." – *Midwest Book Review*

Lee Lynch

"Lynch, with a dozen novels to her credit dating back to the early days of Naiad Press, has earned her stripes as a writerly elder. She was contributing stories to the lesbian magazine *The Ladder* four decades ago. But this latest is sublimely in tune with the times." – *Q-Syndicate*

JLee Meyer

"*Forever Found*…neatly combines hot sex scenes, humor, engaging characters, and an exciting story." – *MegaScene*

Radclyffe

"…well-plotted…lovely romance…I couldn't turn the pages fast enough!" – Ann Bannon, author of *The Beebo Brinker Chronicles*

Susan Smith

"This disparate duo's lush rush of a romance—which incorporates reincarnation, a grounded transman and his peppy daughter, and the dark moods of a troubled witch—pays wonderful homage to Leslie Feinberg's classic gender-bending novel, *Stone Butch Blues*." – *Q-Syndicate*

Ali Vali

"Rich in character portrayal, *The Devil Inside* by Ali Vali is an unusual, unpredictable, and thought-provoking love story that will have the reader questioning the definition of right and wrong long after she finishes the book." – *JustAboutWrite*

LEARNING CURVE

by
Rachel Spangler

2008

LEARNING CURVE

ISBN 10: 1-60282-001-5
ISBN 13: 978-1-60282-001-2

This Trade Paperback Original Is Published By
Bold Strokes Books, Inc.,
New York, USA

First Edition: January 2008

CREDITS
Editors: Jennifer Knight and Stacia Seaman
Production Design: Stacia Seaman
Cover Design By Sheri (graphicartist2020@hotmail.com)

Acknowledgments

Thank you first of all to Radclyffe for allowing me to live this dream. You have created the ideal environment for a young author to thrive. To the rest of the Bold Strokes family, you have taken me in and shown me unparalleled support through this entire process; you are all amazing. Jennifer Knight and Stacia Seaman, editors extraordinaire, thank you for your insight and guidance in helping to make this final product better than I could have ever imagined. Sheri, your covers are always stellar, and I am honored to have one associated with my writing.

There is another group that will probably never fully understand the role they played in the creation of this novel, but they deserve a lot of recognition. While at Illinois State University, I had the great pleasure of working with intelligent, passionate, and giving individuals who all played a role in my development as a person and a writer. I hope I am able to do you justice.

Special acknowledgment also goes out to the Wednesday Night Pedagogy Group. You all are the best. You have encouraged me through each step of creating "the novel." Thank you especially to Lori, who acted as beta reader—*Learning Curve* wouldn't be the same without her contributions.

From day one my family has been my biggest advocate. I know you haven't always understood where I was going, but you have always been there with never-ending amounts of love and support. I cannot thank you enough for giving me the strength to be the person I am finally becoming.

Finally, my eternal gratitude goes to my wife, Susie. This book is yours as much as it is mine. Your love inspired me to write, your encouragement gave me the will to push forward, your faith in me instilled the confidence to share my work with the world. I will never be able to express how much you mean to me, but I am going to spend the rest of my life trying, come what may.

Dedication

For Susie. It's all your fault!

CHAPTER ONE

Ashton Clarke moved smoothly through the sea of swaying bodies. Music pounded through large speakers hanging from each wall of the Triangle Club. Strobe lights flashed a rainbow of rapidly changing hues, giving the dance floor a psychedelic resemblance to a life-size kaleidoscope. She was wearing a loose-fitting pair of faded blue jeans and a skintight black T-shirt that hugged every muscle in her torso. As she wove her way across the room and up to the bar, in a single glance, she took in her surroundings and the women rocking to the beat. Quite a crowd for a Thursday night in Roosevelt, Ohio.

"*Hola*, Pantalona," she greeted the soft butch behind the bar.

Lupe was probably in her early fifties but looked older. The corners of her mouth were creased from years of smoking, and flecks of gray speckled her close-cut dark hair. Lines rimmed her sparkling eyes, a product of her frequent and hearty laugh. She gave a slight bow and replied, "*Buenas noches,* Don Juana."

Ash perched herself on an empty stool and slapped her hand on the bar. "Hey, Lupe, one bottle of Corona, and don't forget my lime."

"My, my, someone's feeling festive tonight."

"You betcha. It's a gorgeous night, I've got money in my pocket, and I'm surrounded by beautiful women."

The bartender snapped the top off a bottle of Corona. "Ah, looking for a wife for the night?"

"Who isn't?" Ash laughed. "A Miss Right Now would suit me just fine."

"Well, not that you heard it from me, but there's a hot mamacita checking you out from over in the corner."

Ash didn't even look. "The femme in the short red dress?"

"Damn, how did you know?"

"I noticed her when I came in. What's she drinking?"

The bartender indicated Ash's Corona.

Ash grinned. "Well then, my friend, make that two Coronas."

A moment later, drinks in hand, Ash strolled toward the dark-haired beauty sitting alone at a tall table in the corner of the bar. She looked the woman up and down, letting her eyes travel up a pair of deeply tanned legs and a smooth torso to the soft curve of her breast, past her slender neck and full lips, right into her coffee-colored eyes. Ash felt her libido kick into overdrive as the woman held her stare and gave a subtle nod of recognition.

"I'll trade you a drink for a seat," Ash said.

"That sounds fair," the woman replied. "I'm Rita."

"Ah, lovely Rita, meter maid." Ash claimed the seat next to her. "Is that a family name or was your father a Beatles fan?"

"My mother was the Beatles fan." Rita's gaze drifted from Ash's mouth to her chest, in a blatant appraisal of her physical attributes. "And you? Do you have a name?"

"Ashton Clarke at your service, but you can call me Ash."

"Is that what you tell all the girls?" Rita asked coyly.

"No, not the girls, only the beautiful women."

"Well then, I have no choice but to be complimented."

Ash waited patiently as they made small talk for a few minutes and sipped their drinks. Then she leaned closer and fixed her eyes intently on Rita's. "Lovely Rita, may I ask you a personal question?"

"Of course."

Ash smiled to herself. This woman was falling right into the palm of her hand. "Would you like to dance with me?"

Rita smiled broadly. "I thought you'd never ask."

Ash led tonight's easy conquest out onto the crowded dance floor. The song was fast and they started to move to the beat, eyes locked. They moved closer as the song continued, so close Ash could feel the heat of Rita's body mingling with her own. She could take her in her arms anytime now; she knew Rita wanted her. But she wanted to make sure Rita knew it, too, so she waited. Rita could come to her.

As one song faded into another, Rita finally stepped in, placing a hand on Ash's shoulder and aligning their bodies. Ash slipped her arm around Rita's waist and applied some gentle pressure to the small of her back. Their movements coincided beautifully and Ash slid one of her knees between Rita's legs and gently rocked back and forth to the beat. Rita let out a small moan and clung tightly to Ash's neck, breathing faster. Ash held back, not wanting to give in to the urge too soon. She felt Rita sigh at the withdrawal.

Just then the music slowed. A soft ballad wafted through the room. Confident that she had Rita right where she wanted her, Ash slowly caressed her back through the thin material of her dress. Rita responded with soft kisses. Along her neck, up her jawline, across her cheek. When she began nibbling on her ear, Ash returned the favor, bending down to drag her lips across Rita's neck. Rita turned slightly and their lips met, softly at first, but as the pressure increased, Ash parted her lips and allowed her tongue to flash into Rita's waiting mouth.

It took them a moment to realize the song had ended. Ash opened her eyes slowly to meet a seductive stare.

"Maybe we'd better take a break," Rita said, stepping back.

"Sure, would you like another drink?"

"That'd be wonderful." Rita almost purred. "I'll go freshen up. You get the drinks, and I'll meet you back at the table."

With a grin, Ash walked back to the bar.

"Two Coronas?" Lupe asked.

"Nope, just one. You'd better make mine a Coke."

"A Coke, already?"

Ash nodded. "I think I may need to drive pretty soon."

Lupe popped the top of the Corona and poured a Coke. "You must be on fire tonight."

"When you've got it, you've got it."

"Yeah, yeah, rub it in."

Ash threw a five on the bar and said, "Keep the change."

She and Rita reached their table at the same time. Ash pulled out a chair for her, and then scooted her own in close enough that their legs were touching. Holding her Coke in one hand, she let the other slip from the table to rest gently on Rita's thigh.

"You're a good dancer," Rita said.

"I had a good partner," Ash came back quickly.

Rita studied her as though trying to decide whether she wanted to take the next step. Ash had seen this situation enough to know the woman's mind was likely telling her to be cautious, while her body was telling her something entirely different.

"You're smooth," Rita said. "I don't know whether to be flattered or suspicious."

"You're in control of this situation. I'm following your lead here," Ash answered, but at the same time she fingered the hem of Rita's dress, making it ride up slightly on her thigh.

"So if I wanted to shake hands and say good night right now, you wouldn't try to stop me?"

"Not at all." Ash leaned in and whispered in her ear. "But I don't think that's what you really want." She could feel Rita softening to her touch, so she continued moving her hand slowly up her thigh. "I think you want the same thing I do, but I'm going to leave that up to you. We could talk, we could dance, we could say good night right now." She paused for emphasis and felt Rita's body rise and fall with each breath she took. "Or we could move on to something else, but the choice is yours."

She allowed her words to linger a second, then sat back,

breaking all contact between their bodies. As she took a long drink of her Coke, she watched Rita's face, reading the mix of doubt and lust that battled within her, each emotion trying to steer the night in opposite directions. Ash waited patiently. She didn't have anything to worry about. She knew exactly what the end result would be. There was no need to force the issue.

She finally got the green light she'd been waiting for when Rita set her drink firmly on the table and asked, "Your place or mine?"

Ash struggled to keep her balance as they fumbled up the stairs to Rita's apartment while simultaneously undressing each other. They paused only long enough for Rita to unlock the door, then rushed inside, kicking off their shoes and stumbling over to the couch.

"The bedroom's on the other side of the kitchen," Rita said breathlessly.

"That's too far away." Ash buried her face in the nape of Rita's neck. "I'm going to take you right here."

Their already scarce clothing gave way to bare skin as Ash pulled the appropriate strings on Rita's dress and it fell to the floor. She kissed Rita's lips before allowing her mouth to travel down her neck and over her shoulder. Just as she was about to take a dark nipple in her mouth, Rita sat up and pushed her down backward on the couch. She tugged at Ash's belt and then the buttons on her jeans. As soon as she slid these over Ash's hips, she lifted her hands to Ash's face. For a moment, she gazed into her eyes, then she ran her fingertips up through Ash's hair.

Ash closed her eyes, surrendering to the physical. No more need for thinking, no more calculations, there was nothing left to do but react. Her pulse quickened and her breathing became more shallow as Rita softly caressed a path down her chest and abdomen, teasing the sensitive flesh. As she inched down, Ash felt her body tighten, her muscles contracting with anticipation and arousal. When Rita zeroed in on her thighs, Ash rolled over, and they tumbled onto the floor. She swiftly took Rita's wrists in one of her hands and held them over her head.

"So you like to tease?" she whispered in Rita's ear. "Then turnabout is fair play."

She ran her tongue down Rita's neck, taking her time, moving steadily downward until she was between the deeply tanned thighs. As she licked and nibbled at the soft flesh, inching ever so slowly toward her target, Rita lifted her hips trying to hasten the process. Each time Ash drew back, she heard a sigh of frustration. She could feel Rita's desire mounting and wanted to keep her on the edge for as long as she could.

Rita clutched at Ash's neck and back. "I can't wait anymore."

"Patience is a virtue, my dear." Ash chuckled softly.

"Please," Rita begged in a moan that was more of a command than a request.

Ash bowed her head, and with a few deliberate flicks of her expert tongue, she felt the woman beneath her shudder as waves of pleasure swept through her body.

"Oh, my God," Rita panted. "That was amazing."

Ash crawled up next to her. "I do what I can."

With a smug grin, she rolled onto her back and closed her eyes, allowing herself to rest for just a moment. When she felt the soft strokes of gentle fingers caress her body, she knew it was going to be a long night.

The bank clock on the street corner flashed 4:23 a.m. as Ash quietly slipped out of Rita's apartment. Stopping to collect the garments scattered on the front steps, she breathed in the crisp fall air and decided she was close enough to walk home. As she trekked through the empty downtown streets, she couldn't help but hum the Beatles' "Lovely Rita." It had been a good night and she looked forward to dreaming about it when she finally crawled into her own bed.

Her large, rustic loft was located above an old warehouse. The space, like the neighborhood, was bare bones, a typical bachelor pad. It was open, uncluttered, and unrefined, and Ash liked it that way. She unlocked the door and crossed through the kitchen and living area on the way to her bed. The light on her answering machine was blinking, and she pushed the button to play her messages as she shed her clothing.

"Ash, it's Mary. Call me when you finally stumble in. Sharon has to work tomorrow, so I thought you might like to join Annie and me at the park. Call me either way and let me know you're home safe. Love you."

Ash smiled and picked up the phone. She had known Mary since they were teenagers. She wasn't sure exactly when her best friend had started checking in on her so frequently, but it happened so often they seemed to take it for granted.

"Hey, Casanova," Mary answered sleepily.

"I'm home safe."

"What time is it?"

"Almost five," Ash said.

"Time to get up."

"Time to go to bed."

"You never cease to amaze me." Mary yawned. "See you at the park at one?"

"We'd better make it two."

"Okay. Love you."

"Love you, too." Ash was asleep almost before she got the phone back on the table.

CHAPTER TWO

Anybody have any thoughts on the 'Oppression' article?" Carrie Fletcher scanned her class.

The students, mostly sophomores and juniors, avoided making eye contact with her, not a promising sign. It could be that this was a Friday morning during the first week of classes and they weren't awake yet. More likely, most had just failed to read the article. This was a general education class, so many of the students were only present to fulfill a requirement and not because of a genuine interest in women's studies.

"I don't need any major revelations, just your reactions to the piece." Carrie wasn't going to let them off the hook. She could wait as long as they could.

After a long silence, a young woman in the front row raised her hand. "I liked the birdcage analogy."

The student wore jeans that fit her loosely and a shirt that covered her midriff. She leaned forward attentively and the copy of the article she had on her desk was heavily highlighted with numerous notes in the margins. *She's going to be one of my good ones*, Carrie thought. In every class, there were always one or two who showed up fully engaged in the subject matter. They could be counted on to bring some insight to the discussion.

"The birdcage analogy is a good starting point for us," Carrie said. "What does the author talk about?"

"She says that if a bird were just to look at one wire of its cage, it would never understand why it can't get out. It's only when the bird can see how all the wires are connected that the cage can be processed as a whole." The student paused. "She says that's why women are able to be oppressed. They see each little thing individually and don't see the big picture."

"Very good." Carrie picked up a marker and drew a line on the dry-erase board. "What are some of the individual wires the author mentions?"

"Women make less money than men," someone said.

Carrie labeled the line "gender wage gap," and drew another. "What else?"

"Domestic violence."

Carrie kept drawing lines and labeling them based on the students' answers until she had drawn an entire cage.

"You see," she said, facing the class. "Anyone could get out of an abusive relationship, if most things were running in her favor, and anyone could move out of a low-paying job if other resources were available to her. It's only when many factors come together in the same place at the same time that we have a real system of oppression strong enough to hold women down."

"Bad things happen to everyone," a girl defiantly said from the back of the room. "Some people just complain too much."

There she is, Carrie thought. The girl was wearing a tight sorority sweater that showed way too much skin to actually provide any warmth, and her skirt was so short that Carrie was afraid to look too closely. The student didn't have anything on her desk to take notes with. Instead she was slouched back in her chair with her arms folded across her chest. Every class had its malcontent, a student convinced from day one that the class was full of evil feminists out to brainwash her. They were usually lost causes, and keeping them from derailing the discussion could cost a lot of class time.

"That's true," Carrie said carefully. She had to set a

professional but nonthreatening tone, if not for this student, then for the rest of the class. The worst thing she could do was become snide or sarcastic. That would only confirm the stereotype about feminists being bitchy, and might prevent other students from speaking freely about other contentious topics in the future. Credibility was key, and she couldn't afford to lose it for any reason. "The author discusses this in the article, remember?"

When the student glared at her instead of responding, Carrie continued. "She gives the example of the rich guy who is on a ski vacation and falls and breaks his leg. Now that's unfortunate, and it probably hurts quite a bit. An injury like that will definitely slow him down, but is it oppression?"

When a student in the middle of the classroom shook his head slightly, Carrie asked him, "Why not?"

He flushed slightly, looking nervous about being called on. He appeared to be a typical college male, in jeans and a T-shirt, with unruly curls sticking out from underneath a tattered baseball cap.

"Because it was just a one-time thing," he answered.

Carrie could see that he'd been taking notes and also had the article out on his desk, so she decided to nudge him into a more complex answer. "What does the temporary nature of the event have to do with oppression?"

"Well," he looked down at his notes as if willing the answer to pop out of them, "I guess for something to really be oppression, it has to be part of something bigger, not just an accident, but something that happens as part of a whole system. Like that cage you drew?"

"Excellent," Carrie responded. While his answer lacked confidence, it was sincere and thoughtful. *He's my guy*, she thought. He would represent that silent majority that made up middle-class America, neither hostile nor eager. He might become a teacher, or a local politician, or maybe just a father to the next generation. He represented the future, and she had sixteen weeks to reach him, sixteen weeks to inform the way he viewed the world around him.

It wouldn't be easy, especially in a department that was understaffed and underfunded. She'd have no support from the administration, which consisted solely of stuffy old white men, or from the campus climate that glorified drinking, sports, and sex. To compound the situation, she was teaching two other classes, advising several student groups, and working on her own scholarship in an attempt to gain tenure in a highly adversarial environment. Still, she'd entered teaching for the possibility of changing lives and, by extension, changing the world. She carried that goal with her every time she stepped into a classroom. Distractions abounded in the university setting, but she couldn't afford to let anything take away from her interactions with her students. She had sixteen weeks to shape the future, and that was exactly what this group of students represented.

"Come on Ash, don't be such a bad-ass. You'd be great at the center," Mary said as Ash gently pushed the toddler on the swing in front of her. "Just look at how good you are with Annie."

"That's different." Ash glanced at her best friend.

Mary Saban was short with blond hair she kept cut neatly at shoulder length. She'd put on a few pounds over the decade since Ash first met her, and had also taken to wearing the denim jumpers that seemed to come with her job as an elementary teacher. She had a contagious smile and an energy that seemed to radiate from every pore. Mary and Ash could not have been more opposite, but perhaps that was what made their friendship so perfect.

"Why is it so different?" Mary asked. "They're still just kids."

"Well, those 'kids' at the center are teenagers, and the last thing I want to do is contribute to the delinquency of minors."

It was a beautiful day for a stroll in the park. The warmth of the sun was only slightly offset by a cool autumn breeze. After the night she'd had, Ash was glad Mary's daughter, Annie, had opted for a mindless activity when they reached the children's play area. All she had to do was remember to push the swing when it slowed.

"Why are you fighting this so hard? You were in their place not that many years ago," Mary said.

"Yeah, and I made it just fine without any gay and lesbian youth groups to coddle me." Noting the dejected look on her best friend's face, Ash added more softly, "I'm sorry, but I'm just not a role model."

"You were a role model to me."

"And look how you turned out," Ash teased. "You broke my heart, settled down, and started a family. I thought I could make a player out of you, but all you wanted was respectability."

"You helped me through a tough time, and you did a great job. I think you could do the same thing for some of the kids at the center."

"You want me to sleep with *them*?"

"Oh my God, no!" Mary blushed. "You can't do *exactly* what you did with me, but you could show them that it's okay for them to just be who they are."

Ash lifted Annie from the swing and put her back in her stroller, carefully fastening the straps. "Mommy is just not giving up on this one, kiddo."

Mary tried one more time. "Just come to the meeting tomorrow, and then if you still don't want to do it, I won't bring it up again."

"Promise?"

"I promise."

"All right, Annie, you heard her. One meeting and she'll drop it."

The toddler smiled and nodded as she usually did when she heard her name.

"Okay, you win," Ash said. "I'll go tomorrow. But it's the only Saturday night I'm giving up."

"Thanks, Ash, and the kids have to be home by eleven, so we can still hit the Triangle Club afterward. I'll even buy you a beer."

"Miss Mary at a bar? What will your wife say?" Ash mocked.

"She trusts us. Besides, I've been home all summer. She can handle Annie on her own for a few hours. And by the way, she thinks coming to the center would be good for you, too."

"Good for me how?" Ash raised an eyebrow.

"You need something stable in your life."

"I thought you were my stability."

"Just come. Okay?"

Heaving a protracted sigh, Ash picked up her old leather jacket, stroked Annie's soft blond hair, and kissed Mary on the cheek. "I'll be there at seven."

As she strode toward her car, she regretted caving in. She was a pushover when it came to Mary, but the gay and lesbian youth center was not her idea of a good time. The thought of coddling a bunch of kids who needed to be babied through the coming-out process didn't appeal to her at all. She found the whole concept silly. She hadn't needed any role models, and she certainly couldn't see herself playing that part for someone else.

After leaving the park, Ash headed downtown and pulled into the parking lot of a small gray building labeled Mick's Mechanics. She rolled down her car window and shouted "Hey" to a red-haired man with his head under the hood of an old Cadillac. "You got an open lift?"

Mick Darby stood up and wiped his hand on his jeans. He was about twenty-five years old, but still had a bit of a baby face.

His hair was tousled, and it looked like someone had taken a dirty cloth and smudged grease and oil randomly across his arms, face, and clothes.

He grinned broadly at Ash. "For you, anything. Pull on around."

Ash drove the Mustang into the big bay door he rolled open for her and pulled slowly forward until he motioned for her to stop. She hopped out of the car and tossed her jacket into the front seat.

"How's business?" she asked as she walked over and flipped a lever on the wall. The lift climbed up out of the floor and made contact with the frame of her car, raising it ever so slightly.

"I can't complain." Mick closed the hood of the car he'd been working on and took a seat on a nearby stool. "That transmission you sent me last week was quite a piece of work."

"If you thought the car was a piece of work, you should have seen the owner." Ash rolled up her sleeves and checked to make sure the lift had hit squarely on the Mustang's frame.

She and Mick had a deal. She got to use his shop and tools for her car care projects, and in return she sent him any major repairs she couldn't handle on her own.

He shook his head. "It figures."

"What?" Ash levered the car high enough that she could stand beneath it, then rolled an oil pan under with her.

"You get laid, and all I get is a busted transmission."

Ash threw back her head and laughed. "Yeah, I guess I did get the better end of that deal."

She took a socket wrench from an open toolbox, gave the drain plug a good twist, and then reached up to remove the plug by hand. The minute the plug was out, a steady stream of oil ran into the drain pan. Ash moved out from under the car and leaned against a workbench to watch the process.

"She's beautiful," Mick said, admiring her ride.

The red '64 Mustang convertible was flawless. Ash had

taken the time to rebuild the engine herself, using only original parts. She then searched all over to find the perfect shade of burnt red to match the original color and personally oversaw the paint job. It had been a three-year labor of love but the end product was enough to make any car junkie drool. In fact, Mick looked like he was on the verge of drooling at that very moment.

"How much would you want for her?" he asked.

"Not a chance, buddy." Ash returned to the Mustang with an oil filter wrench in hand. "There's no way I'm selling her. This car is a chick magnet. We're a team."

Mick rolled his eyes. "Like you need any help. I've never set foot in a gay bar and even *I* know your reputation."

"I don't know what you're talking about." Ash feigned innocence as she unscrewed the oil filter and allowed the excess fluid to drain into the pan.

Mick mumbled something about her being a poster girl for the love-'em-and-leave-'em lifestyle and she threw her grease rag at him.

"Yeah? And where's your wedding ring?"

"Fair enough." He smiled. "I'm in no hurry to settle down, either. All I'm saying is you don't need the car to pick up women."

"Probably not, but she's still fun to drive."

After wiping out the filter ring, Ash dipped a finger in the oil pan and coated the gasket of the new filter seal before twisting it into place and screwing the drain plug back in. She rolled the drain pan out from under the car and lowered the lift. Mick handed her a few quarts of oil.

"Got a funnel?" she asked, popping the hood.

"No, we used them all at the wild kegger we had last night," Mick answered sarcastically. He tossed her a plastic funnel.

When she was done and had checked the oil level with a dipstick, she closed the hood and shook Mick's hand. "Thanks for the lift."

"You know you can use the shop anytime," he said as she slid back into the Mustang. "But do me a favor. Next time you send me a blown transmission, just make sure you send the girl with it."

Ash just smiled as she drove away. She wasn't about to make any promises.

CHAPTER THREE

A sh spent most of Saturday trying to come up with an excuse Mary hadn't heard before. When there was something she wanted to avoid, she could get quite original, but her best friend knew her too well to be fooled. In the end, Ash decided her best option was to give in and make an appearance. Mary would be happy she made the effort, but she and everyone else would soon realize Ash was not a positive role model. Hopefully she could slip out early.

It was seven p.m. when she slowed the Mustang to a stop across the street from the gay and lesbian youth center. She took a moment to check out her appearance in the rearview mirror before turning off the engine. She looked like she did on any given day, in jeans and white T-shirt beneath a denim jacket that had seen better days. Her dark brown hair was cut short, giving her a boyish look. Usually she radiated confidence, but tonight she had to take a deep breath before getting out of the car. She strode across the street, but as she reached the door a group of teenage girls pushed through from the other side.

Ash stepped back to let them pass. They were bantering among themselves and paid no attention to her. One paused briefly and flashed what appeared to be a practiced smile before moving on. She looked as tempting as she was young. Her blond hair was pulled into a ponytail threaded through the back of a baseball cap. She wore a black sweater and a baggy pair of khakis. She was a few inches shorter than Ash and had to look up to make eye contact, but when she did her eyes flashed a mysterious hazel.

The encounter only lasted a few seconds, but Ash was left shaking her head. She could spot the type from a mile away; she'd wasted too many nights with women who knew their own power but were still learning how to use it. They knew how to get what they wanted but weren't mature enough to know what they needed. They were dangerous and most often more trouble than they were worth.

That kid will break a lot of hearts, especially if she's starting this young, she thought as she entered the building.

The inside of the center looked like a doctor's office waiting room. Several magazine racks lined a narrow foyer just inside the door. These overflowed with pamphlets and gay publications: *The Advocate, Curve, AIDS and You,* not to mention a plethora of safe-sex booklets and brochures. As Ash walked on, the room seemed to widen, opening up to what looked like a large living area furnished with couches and beanbag chairs. A TV stood in the corner, complete with DVD player and video game console. The walls were decorated with modern art and posters, complemented with the occasional photograph of smiling young people, usually clad in rainbow apparel.

Ash couldn't help but wonder how she would have fit into a place like this when she was a teenager. She would probably have been the one who got in trouble for bringing beer or seducing the chaperones. She chuckled at the thought.

"You came!" Mary approached her with a smile.

"I said I would." Ash gave the mandatory three back pats before escaping Mary's hug.

"Well, come and meet everybody." Mary tugged on Ash's arm, and they almost bumped into a group of boys making a mad dash for the video games.

She introduced Ash to several she said were regulars. After

mumbled hellos, the boys slipped past and Mary gestured toward a young man impeccably dressed in khakis and a baby blue polo shirt. His perfectly coiffed hair and emerald green eyes made Ash wonder if he'd been the boy in school pined over hopelessly by all the girls, or the sensitive one picked on by the jocks. Probably a bit of both, she decided.

"This is Michael Hays," Mary said.

Michael shook Ash's hand gently. "It's nice to meet you, finally." With a sly smile, he added, "Your reputation precedes you."

"Oh? Has Mary been telling stories about me?"

"Just a few. She seems enamored with you."

"I tend to have that effect on women."

"So I hear. In fact, I think you've already made quite an impression on one of our other volunteers," Michael replied cattily. "Speak of the devil, here she comes now."

Great! Ash thought. She'd wined and dined her fair share of women but had hardly ever stuck around the next morning, so the reunions were rarely as sweet as the rendezvous themselves. She scanned the woman approaching. In capri pants, a white tank top, and a cut denim jacket, she looked like she'd stepped out of an advertisement for the Gap. Her lips were painted a deep red and her auburn hair was fashioned into a bob that called attention to her bright green eyes. Ash had no trouble figuring out why she'd pursued the redhead; she was attractive and had a good body. But details of the night they'd spent together eluded her. Vague images filled her mind: a bar, drinks, making out in the Mustang, and then at the woman's apartment, where there was more wine and they'd fallen into bed.

She remembered very little about their encounter or the next morning, which probably meant it was exactly like so many others, a good time followed by Ash slipping out of the apartment sometime around the break of dawn.

"Hello, Ash." Her one-night stand smiled but her expression was calculating.

"Hello, uh…" Ash fumbled, unable to come up with a name.

"Amy." The response was supplied with a tinge of irritation.

"Right. So how have you been?" Ash wondered why Mary hadn't stepped in to help her out. Michael also seemed to be enjoying watching her squirm.

"Fine. I'm seeing someone now."

"Great." Ash was relieved. "How's that going?"

"Wonderful. She stays the night and even returns my calls."

Ash grimaced. She'd been in this situation a few times and had learned that the less she said, the better.

"She's working tonight, but maybe she'll be here next Saturday. You could meet her if you stick around long enough."

"Actually, I just came by to see Mary." Ash was ready for the awkward conversation to end. "I'm about to head out."

"Wow, leaving before the party begins? That's not like you."

"Yeah, well, you know, Saturday night." More people were filtering into the center, and Ash figured this would be a good time to escape. It looked like Mary had plenty of help and would not need an extra adult. "I should get going. Good to see you again, Amy, and congratulations on the girlfriend." After a polite farewell to Michael, she nudged Mary. "Will you walk me out?"

Mary didn't answer. She was busy exchanging glowing smiles with one of the new arrivals. Ash followed the direction of her gaze and saw what she truly believed to be the most breathtaking woman she'd ever laid eyes on. Not supermodel beautiful, but cool, real, understated beauty. She looked like one of those women who have it all together. She was almost as tall as Ash, with long brown curls cascading over slender shoulders. She was sleek without being thin and carried herself with gentle poise, sinewy limbs accenting her soft curves. Her body was highly sexual, yet Ash was startled to find she instantly saw more than a woman she would want to hit on. Something in her reaction transcended lust. Confused, she had to fight to maintain her composure as a pair of soft blue eyes took her in briefly. The woman gave a polite smile that seemed heartbreakingly sweet.

"You must be Ash," she said, extending her hand. "Mary talks about you all the time."

Warm fingers firmly encircled Ash's, giving a brief, steady squeeze. *Who is this woman, and how have I never met her before?* She felt exposed, sure that everyone in the room could tell she was taken aback. It was unusual that a woman was able to catch her off guard, and Ash wasn't sure if she liked the sensation.

"Meet Carrie Fletcher," Mary cut in. "I was just about to ask Ash to stay for the meeting tonight, Carrie."

For a moment Ash had forgotten everything around them. As she came back to reality, she remembered Michael and Amy and the whole awkward situation she'd been fleeing.

"Oh, you weren't leaving, were you?" Carrie sounded genuinely regretful.

Ash glanced at Amy, who was standing with her arms folded across her chest. She knew she should get out while she could, but when she met Carrie's gaze once more she realized she wasn't going anywhere. "I was planning on it. But if you all would like some help here tonight, I guess I could stick around."

"Wonderful." Another sweet smile lit Carrie's face. "I'd really like you to meet my neighbor Tess. She's a good kid, but a handful. Mary was saying you might be just the person to get through to her."

I don't want to get through to anyone but you right now. With a quick glare at Mary, Ash said, "Well, I'm not really good with kids."

In the background, Amy remarked, "She and Tess are two of a kind. They deserve each other."

Ash wondered what that was supposed to mean. She didn't

have to wonder long. The group of girls she'd seen leaving earlier had walked back in. She wouldn't have noticed them except for the quick flash of tenderness in Carrie's eyes. Ash's heart sank when she realized which of the group had elicited this response—the blond teen who'd cruised her outside the center. How could a woman like Carrie be interested in a girl like that? Anyone could see she was nothing but trouble, not to mention that she couldn't be a day over sixteen.

"Ladies, come here," Mary said in perfect schoolteacher tone. "I want you to meet Ashton. She's going to be helping out tonight." She started reeling off names.

"I'm Tess," the blonde interrupted.

"Ah, Tess the infamous." Ash wished she could avoid shaking hands but Tess wouldn't have it.

"So, you're here to help give us the safe sex talk for the millionth time?" she said, stroking Ash's wrist.

"The what?" Ash hoped she'd misheard. She tugged her hand away, trying to seem casual while determined to stay in control of the situation.

With a flip of her ponytail, Tess said, "Or perhaps you're here because Mary thinks you could benefit from the lesson as well." She moved past Ash without waiting for a reply, and the other girls followed their femme fatale.

Ash knew she'd been caught off guard and therefore lost her high ground. To Mary, she said, "Safe sex night? You've got to be joking."

Mary shrugged off her protest. "It's only a small part of the meeting. We have to do it once a month to keep our state funding. You don't have to say a word."

"Mary, you need to 'fess up now. Any more surprises coming for me tonight? Anything else you forgot to mention?"

"Ash, I'm sorry. I should have warned you."

"About which part? Amy, the ex-fling? Or Tess, the young seductress?" Ash spoke in a raspy whisper, trying to hide her anger from anyone else who might be listening. "Was the sex education class a special bonus?"

"If I'd told you about everything, you wouldn't have come."

"Damn right I wouldn't have."

"But you're here now, so grow up and act like an adult. Or throw a temper tantrum and look more immature than the kids. The choice is yours."

Mary stomped off, leaving Ash standing there with her mouth open. She'd known her best friend long enough to understand she only got snippy when it was deserved. Mary had put up with a lot from her over the past decade. First, the philandering during the brief time they'd been lovers in their late teens. Then Ash's party-every-night mentality in their early twenties, followed by her snide attitude about Mary's desire to settle down and raise a family. Through it all Mary had been patient and understanding, loving Ash for who she was.

With a sigh, Ash trudged to the area where the others were taking seats in a haphazard circle of chairs and beanbags. She scanned the room for the evening's one redeeming factor, but Carrie was already sitting next to one of the girls. Ash picked up a chair and carried it over.

"Do you mind?" she asked, flashing a smile.

"Not at all." Carrie smiled back. "It looks like Michael wants to get started."

Ash placed the chair next to Carrie, on the side no one had taken. As she sat, she let herself breathe in the sweet scent of Carrie's shampoo. It wasn't overpowering, just a subtle hint of soap and citrus. She wondered how it would feel to run her fingers through those soft-looking dark curls. She was so engrossed she didn't even notice Tess take the seat directly opposite her in their untidy circle.

Michael called the room to attention, reminding everyone, "It's that time of the month again."

The teens in the room let out a collaborative groan, and one of the girls said, "You can only show us STD charts so many times before we just go numb."

Ash couldn't help but chuckle. She wouldn't want to have sex education lessons from Michael either.

Amy stood up, taking over the reins. "Let's talk about lesbian sex tonight." The boys breathed a sigh of relief, and the girls grumbled among themselves. "What questions do you have? You know you can ask us anything."

"I have a question," Tess announced.

The room became quiet. Ash got the feeling Amy was about to be ambushed. *Serves her right*, she thought. She sure didn't remember Amy being all that serious about safe sex the night they'd spent together.

Amy grimaced. "What can I help you with?"

"Actually, my question is for Ash."

Ash whipped her head up. Tess was calling her out. She supposed she should have seen it coming.

"Ashton is just observing this evening," Amy said without warmth. "But I'm sure any of the other volunteers would be happy to field your question."

Ash's blood surged within her. She was being challenged, not only by Tess but by Amy as well. They were both betting she couldn't handle the question that hadn't even been asked yet. Refusing to be intimidated by a teenager and a woman she wished she'd never slept with, she said, "No, that's okay, Tess. Go ahead."

She was aware of the tension pulling at her from each side of the room. The adults seemed to be bracing themselves for an impending train wreck, and the teens all teetered on their seats as if anticipating a fight in the school yard.

"I was just wondering if you practice safe sex." Tess grinned, making it clear that she was baiting the new adult in the discussion.

Ash reviewed her options. If she said yes, she was one of

the adults, and a liar at that. If she said no, she was irresponsible and would be seen as a bad role model by the other volunteers. Finally, she could refuse to answer, but that would make her a prude at the same time implying guilt. She'd been put in a lose/lose situation.

"Well, it really depends on what you mean by safe sex. If you're asking me if I use dental dams, the answer is usually not." She tried not to look at the horror on the faces of the various adults in the room. Next to her, she felt Carrie tense up. "However, that doesn't mean I'm stupid."

"Uh-huh." A smug expression crept across Tess's features.

"I never go home with someone I don't know unless I tell someone where I'm going and when I intend to get home. I always have enough money in my pocket for a cab fare. And I never have sex when I've had so much to drink that I'm not in control of the situation. The minute anyone tries to pressure me into doing something I'm not comfortable with, the evening is over, no exceptions. And by the way, that's not just for lesbians. You guys should hold yourselves to the same standards."

Ash allowed herself to look around the room. No one was laughing or rolling their eyes. Most were nodding as if her words registered.

"What if you try to say no to something and the other person gets offended?" a boy asked.

"That's what the cab fare is for."

All the kids laughed at that.

On a more serious note, Ash said, "Anyone who won't put their lover at ease is probably going to be a selfish lay anyway."

She noticed Tess's smile had changed from one of triumph to one of reluctant appreciation. Carrie was right, the girl was a handful. Ash had the impression she was used to controlling the people around her by whatever means were at her disposal. She knew how to command attention, and judging by her looks and demeanor, she was used to getting a lot of it.

For the next twenty minutes or so, the adults led a discussion about dealing with peer pressure, then Mary said, "All right, if there are no more questions, I think that's a good place to wrap up."

After the teens had left the circle for their activities of choice, Ash stood and stretched her legs. She hadn't noticed how tense her muscles were. Mary was wrapped up in a conversation and Ash couldn't see where Carrie had gone. Trying to kill time, she watched the boys play a video game but she didn't understand the concept and the graphics made her dizzy. She moved to a table where several girls were flipping through the latest issue of *Curve,* trying to decide which lesbian starlet they would rather date. After a few minutes she became bored with their discussion and decided to duck out of the center to catch some fresh air. The evening had taken on a surreal feeling and it was only nine p.m.

Ash ambled across the street to her car and rested her back against the driver's side door. For a moment she allowed her mind to drift but she snapped back to reality when she felt someone approaching. She almost groaned out loud when she saw Tess crossing the street, her freshly glossed lips curved in a seductive smile. The predatory look gave Ash a chill, but she didn't know exactly why.

"Got a cigarette?" Tess asked coyly.

"No."

"What? The big, bad Ash doesn't smoke?"

"No."

"What's with the one-word answers all of a sudden? You didn't seem too reserved before."

"You didn't come out here for a cigarette," Ash replied flatly.

Tess gave a brief pause as if weighing her next move. Ash watched as she shifted gears.

"A muscle car, huh?" She ran her fingertips up the hood of the Mustang. "That's pretty predictable, don't you think?"

"What you see is what you get, sweetheart."

"Really?" Tess moved closer, well into Ash's personal space.

Ash was determined not to take a step away. The best way to keep control around people like Tess was to hold her ground.

"I don't know," Tess continued. "The car could be a complement to you, but then again it could just be overcompensation."

"I've never had any complaints." Ash cursed herself as soon as the words left her mouth. Her reply had sounded like a come-on, playing into the sexual tension Tess was trying to create.

"No, I guess you wouldn't." Tess lifted her hand from the car and encircled her fingers around Ash's bicep. "Muscle car, muscle dyke?"

In an instant Ash clasped Tess's wrist and plucked the hand away. But instead of releasing it, she pulled Tess closer, leaning down so her mouth was next to the girl's ear. Thinking she was about to be kissed, Tess closed her eyes and tilted her chin upward.

"Listen up, kid," Ash whispered in her ear. "You are playing way out of your league. You're just lucky I am who I am, and not someone who would take advantage of a kid trying to play temptress."

Tess's eyes shot open. "Let go of me."

She started to pull away, but Ash held her more firmly. "You had better be real careful, because the next person you pull that shit with might just take you for more than you bargained for. Got it?"

Tess looked utterly indignant. Obviously she wasn't used to being talked to like that. Ash released her grip. Out of the corner of her eye, she saw Mary and Carrie staring from across the street. Ash realized immediately that from where they were standing, it must have looked like she was about to kiss Tess.

Tess followed her gaze, and a slow smile settled across her

face. Her composure regained, she spun on her heel and walked past the adults back into the center. Carrie went after her while Mary walked briskly toward Ash.

"What was that all about?"

"Oh, Tess and I were just having a heart-to-heart." Ash tried not to appear shaken by the confrontation.

"Ash, it didn't look good."

"Come on. Mary, you're the one who brought me here in the first place, and now you are trying to accuse me of—"

"I didn't accuse you of anything. You know I trust you."

"Good."

"Let's go back in. Less than two hours left."

Ash assessed her situation. The teens couldn't care less whether she stayed or not, and Mary would soon start making her rounds, checking in with all the kids one on one before the end of the evening. The other adults weren't really interested in talking to her and, besides, they were meant to be there for the kids. She was about to tell Mary she'd rather go home and they could go out to the bar some other time when she glimpsed Carrie passing the open doorway.

"All right, I'll stay awhile longer," she said. "But only for you."

Carrie sat at a table across the room with stacks of papers spread out in front of her. Gathering herself, Ash exhaled and walked over, willing her to look up. She didn't.

"Anyone else sitting here?" she asked.

"No, have a seat," Carrie replied with a smile that almost brought Ash to her knees.

An awkward moment of silence followed, and Carrie looked back at the stacks of papers. Ash's mind ran wild as she tried to think of something clever to say to break the ice. "If I'm interrupting something I can leave you alone."

"No. I was just looking at some student papers, but they're depressing me too much for a Saturday night." She put her pen down and pushed a curl from her forehead. "So, what do you think of the center?"

"Oh, it's great," Ash lied.

"Hmm, not very convincing."

"I'm sorry, I'm really just here because Mary asked me to come. I'm not very comfortable with teenagers."

Carrie laughed. "Don't feel bad. Teenagers aren't very comfortable with other teenagers, either."

"Yeah?" Ash saw a shimmer of hope. Carrie's laugh was intoxicating and the fact that she had been the one to spark it bolstered her confidence. "Then why are you spending your Saturday night reading papers from teenagers in a youth center full of them?"

"Good question." Carrie smiled again. "The papers are from college students, so they aren't exactly teenagers in the conventional sense of the word, although they can be every bit as frustrating."

"You teach college?" Ash asked, getting nervous. She was usually better with women when she could keep the conversation on superficial topics, and college was something she knew nothing about.

"Don't make it sound so scary."

"Sorry." Trying to recover quickly, Ash asked, "What do you teach?"

"Women's studies."

"No kidding? That just happens to be my specialty," Ash said, leaning in closer.

"Really? Well, the papers are on Judith Butler, so you can imagine how my sophomore boys feel about *Undoing Gender*."

"Actually, I was joking. I'm a lesbian, so 'studying women' is kind of what I do." Ash laughed nervously as she realized she'd made Carrie uncomfortable.

"Oh, I guess I walked right into that one."

"No, I'm sorry. That was pretty sophomoric of me. Maybe I should see if any of your students would take me to a frat party." When the beginnings of a genuine smile started to form around the corners of Carrie's mouth, Ash continued, "Really, they could teach me about *Undoing Gender*, and I could teach them how to tap a keg."

"I think they probably know how to tap a keg," Carrie replied good-naturedly. "Surely you have something else to teach them."

"Hmm…do you think they know how to mix drinks?"

"Not very well, if the parties I went to in college are any indication."

"Well, there you go. I could be a professor of the bartending sciences." Ash sensed Carrie relaxing.

"Is that what you do? Tend bar?"

"No, actually I just work odd jobs. I'm a regular Ms. Fix-it. Minor stuff mostly. Painting, refinishing, day-to-day car care."

"That's great. Not many women in that field. How did you get started?"

Ash saw an opening and before she thought her words through, her Casanova instincts took hold of her. "I learned early on that I was good with my hands. Maybe I could show you sometime."

Immediately Carrie tensed up. She wasn't exactly cold, but Ash knew she'd pushed too far, so she tried to cover quickly. "I redid Mary's attic. I'm sure she wouldn't mind showing it to you."

"That would be nice. Maybe I can see it at the cookout tomorrow."

"You're coming to Mary and Sharon's cookout?"

"Of course. I try to bring Tess to all the youth center functions." Ash must have looked a bit off kilter because Carrie seemed to realize she didn't know what was going on. "I'm sure Mary just forgot to mention who all was going to be there."

"Yeah, Mary has a very selective memory." Ash tried to laugh, even though she'd been suckered into another night with Amy, Michael, and of course Tess. *Oh, well, if I have to deal with them to get time with Carrie, I guess I can even handle Tess.*

As if on cue Tess seemed to materialize out of nowhere and sat down directly across the table from her. Ash had been so engrossed in Carrie that she didn't even notice the teenager approaching.

"So where's the after-party?" Tess asked.

"This is it as far as you're concerned," Ash replied.

"What about you? Where are you headed?"

"Sorry, kiddo, nowhere you can go."

"You'd be surprised the places I can find my way into."

"Yeah, and does your mother know where you are right now?"

"Does yours?" Tess shot back.

Ash chuckled at the flash of anger she saw in the girl. "You still can't come."

"Oh, come on. Surely if I was with a local celebrity like yourself I could get in anywhere." Tess batted her eyelashes.

Ash once again felt the urge to snap at Tess, but she could sense Carrie's disapproval. "Probably, but it's almost your bedtime."

"Okay, want to come tuck me in?"

"That's enough," Carrie said sharply. "It's time to go. Why don't you see if anyone else needs a ride home? I'll pack up here."

As Tess reluctantly walked back toward the other girls, Carrie gathered her papers and put them in her briefcase. "I'm sorry about that," she said, without looking up.

Ash felt her heart sink. She was embarrassed about Tess and puzzled that Carrie hadn't stepped in sooner. Carrie seemed disappointed and for some reason that bothered her. She was drawn to this woman in ways she wasn't used to, and while the feeling was unsettling, Ash also found it intriguing. Carrie was beautiful and challenging. Ash had been thoroughly enjoying their conversation and now found herself wanting more.

"Hey, don't worry about it. I shouldn't have let her get me going like that."

"It's not you." Carrie seemed dispirited. "Tess has that effect on people."

"Carrie." Ash touched her lightly on the shoulder. "I'm not most people."

Carrie studied her for a second without saying a word, then picked up her briefcase and said, "I can see that. See you tomorrow."

With that she was gone and Ash was left rocking in her wake.

Chapter Four

D id you girls have fun tonight?" Carrie asked as she drove the car full of teenagers across town. Tess was in the passenger seat next to her looking blankly out the window. Two other teens, Erin and Jill, were in the back and seemed to be in much better moods.

"Oh, yeah." Jill giggled. "I am so glad I came. I finally got to see the famous Ash Clarke."

"She is so hot," Erin jumped in. "Is she going to be there every weekend?"

Carrie shook her head at the clear case of teenage hormones gone haywire. "I got the sense that this was a one-time occurrence, but she might be at the cookout tomorrow."

"Good. Did you think she was hot?" Erin asked Jill.

"She's good-looking, but she's slept with, like, everyone in town."

"So what? When you look like that, you can sleep with pretty much anyone you want."

"Girls, it's not in very good taste to talk about people's private lives," Carrie said gently.

"It's not really a private life if you flaunt it," Erin countered. "My older sister plays softball, and she said Ash has slept with practically everyone on the team. She doesn't even try to hide it."

Carrie couldn't really argue with that logic. Ash's reputation was widely known at the university, too. She'd heard her mentioned by faculty, staff, and students alike, and the story was the same every time. Ash Clarke was a player, the kind of woman who should come with a warning label.

"She's pretty smooth," Erin said.

"She's had lots of practice." Jill snickered at her own retort.

Carrie pulled up to a stoplight and allowed her thoughts to drown out the conversation. They were right, Ash was as smooth as she was stunning. She'd handled Tess's ambush during the safe sex talk pretty well, certainly better than Amy or Michael usually did. And her practiced charm was more than evident when she and Carrie spoke. Carrie wondered if she was even aware that she came on strong really quickly, or if hitting on women was just second nature to her. It was easy to see why some women found that type of confidence attractive, especially younger ones who were also looking for superficial encounters, but that had never been Carrie's style. She'd built her few relationships on common interest and shared respect; sex appeal had always been secondary to her.

Carrie's thoughts were interrupted by the blare of a car horn.

"The light's green," Tess mumbled.

Embarrassed to have zoned out so completely, Carrie focused on the road for the rest of the way to Erin's.

"Are you sure you don't want to spend the night?" Erin asked Tess. "My mom is going to drop me and Jill off at the cookout tomorrow."

"No thanks," Tess said, not really looking at her.

Carrie waited until the girls reached the front door, and pulled away as Erin's mother stepped out on the front porch and waved to her. She and Tess rode in silence for a few moments before she made an attempt at conversation.

"You're awfully quiet all of a sudden."

"Yeah," came Tess's one-word answer.

Carrie knew the teenager didn't want to go home, and she couldn't blame her. Most kids her age fought with their parents from time to time, but Tess and her mother couldn't see eye to eye on anything. She didn't know for sure, but she thought that their house was usually filled with uneasy tension that could explode at any time.

"I'll pick you up for the cookout right after you get home from mass," she said.

"If my mom lets me out of the house."

"Tess, if you behave at mass, your mother will let you go." Carrie pulled into her own driveway.

"Can I come in?" Tess asked without much hope in her voice.

"You know you can't. If you want to keep coming to the youth center, we have to follow your mom's rules, and that means making it home by curfew."

"Whatever." Tess got out of the car and stalked across the street.

No one came onto the porch to welcome her or to wave an acknowledgment to her chaperone. Carrie sighed. The girl's home life was no doubt the cause of her gradual descent into sarcasm and jadedness, but Carrie couldn't do much about a disapproving mother. She just had to try to provide Tess with positive experiences during the time they had together. Mary thought Ash might have something to offer from a different perspective, and even though Carrie was skeptical about that possibility right now, she was willing to try anything.

"Ash," she said out loud.

Now that her chaperoning duties were through for the evening, she could allow her mind to wander to the woman everyone talked about. She was certainly everything her reputation suggested: handsome, charismatic, cocky, and irreverent. Still, there had been moments during their conversation when Carrie thought she'd glimpsed something more—brief flashes of genuine interest, even a hint of sincerity just below Ash's cool exterior. The responses had faded as quickly as they appeared, as if Ash shut down as soon as she became aware she was revealing another part of herself. Carrie would be lying to herself if she said she wasn't intrigued.

❖

Ash took a seat next to Mary at the bar and said, "Amaretto stone sour and a Bud."

"You remembered." Mary leaned into Ash to be heard over the music coursing through the club.

"How could I forget? I'm the one that introduced you to Amaretto. It's what you were drinking the night you left me for Sharon."

Mary seemed shocked. "Ash, there was nothing to leave. We weren't a couple."

"I know. I didn't mean it like that." Ash shook the memory from her mind.

"Something hit a little too close to home?" Mary asked.

"What do you mean?"

"This sudden walk down memory lane, could it have anything to do with Tess?"

"Tess?" Ash tried not to be insulted. She thought Mary knew her better. "I'd never hook up with Tess. She's just a kid, and a troubled one at that."

"Who said anything about hooking up? Are you thinking about sleeping with her?"

"God, no! Do you think I'm so desperate I need to hit on minors?"

Mary took a large swallow from the drink the bartender had placed in front of her. Relaxing noticeably, she said, "You had me worried."

"I thought we were talking about Carrie. I still don't know what Tess has to do with anything," Ash said.

"No, I guess you wouldn't. You've got a one-track mind. I

should have known you would walk into the youth center and find the one woman in this town you hadn't slept with."

"Hey, I'm not that bad. There are a lot of women I haven't slept with."

"Oh, yeah?" Mary laughed. "Point to one."

Ash scanned the crowd on the dance floor. "There. The blonde in the black skirt and red top."

"No, she's too cute. I don't believe you've never gone after her."

"She must be new in town," Ash replied distractedly, never taking her eyes off the woman.

"So, if I ask you tomorrow if you've slept with her your answer will be different?" Mary prodded playfully.

Before Ash could say anything, the blonde saw them watching her and Mary looked away quickly. Ash held the attractive stranger's gaze, giving her a broad smile that was immediately returned.

"Jesus." Mary sighed. "Another one bites the dust."

"All I did was smile at her."

"Exactly. That's all you have to do, flash those pearly whites and women just fall into your arms."

"I'm irresistible." Ash shrugged playfully. "It's my curse."

Mary rolled her eyes. "Oh, you poor thing."

"I really am the victim here."

"A victim with a short attention span at that. What about Carrie? Remember her—the woman you were fawning over all night? Any of this ring a bell?"

"She went home," Ash responded dryly.

"My point exactly." A hint of agitation entered Mary's tone. "Carrie went home, so you just move right on to your next prospect."

Ash was surprised by Mary's expression. She seemed frustrated. "Why are you so concerned about Carrie? And by the way, how come I've never met her before if you two are such good friends?"

"We aren't good friends. We work together on the youth center advisory board, we see each other at all the functions, and we have a shared passion for making this community safe for those kids. I respect her. She believes in things that are bigger than herself."

"And she's sexy."

"Which brings me to my point," Mary said. "It never occurred to me that the two of you should be introduced. You know I love you, but she's not exactly one-night-stand material. Now if you would consider settling down—"

"All right, Mom." Ash feigned exhaustion. "We've been through this a thousand times. I don't want a relationship. I'm not built that way."

"What do you want? Do you even know?"

"Right now I want you to relax, I want another beer, and I want to see if Blondie over there would like to dance with me. But not necessarily in that order."

"Fine." Mary threw up her hands in defeat. "Carrie would never go for you anyway."

They sat there for a moment not saying anything. Ash felt stung by the last remark but tried not to let her feelings show. Somehow being told Carrie was not an option made an ache settle in her chest. She tried to dismiss the thought. There were plenty of other women who would love nothing more than to spend a night with her. She would just have to redirect her attentions to one of them.

All of a sudden Mary said, "I need to get home to Sharon and Annie."

Ash was a bit startled by her abruptness, but when they hugged good-bye, Mary whispered, "Blondie is making her way toward the bar. Call me tomorrow."

Ash laughed at her friend's antics, then ordered another beer. All she had to do now was relax. The blonde would come to her.

❖

The evening progressed rather quickly, even by Ash's standards. She was pleasantly surprised that after only three dances the blonde—Allison—whispered, "I've got a room at the Chateau. If you've got a car here, we can go."

"Are you sure?" Ash eased out of Allison's clinging embrace slightly. She'd been enjoying the ritual of the seduction, but for some reason thoughts of Carrie still lingered in the back of her mind.

"I wouldn't have said it if I wasn't."

"A woman after my own heart." Ash laughed softly, burying her doubts. "Let me pay my tab and we'll go."

Once outside, Ash opened the door of her Mustang for Allison to slide in, then she jogged around to the driver's side. As she did, she had a flashback to earlier that evening, when she and Tess had stood by the car, arguing. She shook her head slightly, wondering what made her think of that.

"This is a great car," Allison remarked as they drove toward the hotel.

"Thanks. She gets me where I want to be." Ash focused her attention on the road. A few seconds later she felt a hand move up her right thigh. She took a deep breath as Allison reached her waist and began to unfasten her belt. "We're almost there," she said hoarsely.

"Good, I don't think I can wait much longer."

"I can see that," Ash said, but in her head she heard Carrie's voice from when she'd used the same words earlier. "Damn," she muttered at the memory.

"What's the matter?" Allison asked, still running her hands over any part of Ash's body she could reach.

"Nothing. Where should I park?"

"By the back door."

As soon as the car was in the space, Ash hurried around to open the passenger side door for Allison and they both bolted for the elevator. By the time the elevator doors opened on the fifth floor, they were latched onto each other, kissing and groping.

Allison had not only made it to second base, she was rounding the corner toward third. A businessman waiting to go downstairs got more than an eyeful before they could tear themselves apart. Neither could refrain from laughing as Allison fumbled with her key, but once the door was opened they were back to business.

Without taking time to bother with the light, Allison backed Ash toward the bed until she was sitting on the edge, and then straddled her leg. Ash pulled her down hard, enjoying the damp warmth resting on her thigh. She ran her hands up under Allison's top and cupped her breasts. Allison moaned deeply.

"Why do I get the feeling you've done this before?" she asked as Ash expertly unhooked the clasps of her bra.

"Probably because you're no rookie, either."

Ash discarded the bra and top, and took a hard nipple between her lips, rolling it around with her tongue. Allison arched her back and ran her fingers through Ash's hair, holding on tightly to keep from falling over backward. She ground her hips down on Ash's knee, moving in slow circles. Her breathing became more ragged with each rotation, making her press down even harder.

"Oh no, you don't," Ash said when she realized how close Allison was to climaxing.

Flipping Allison onto the bed, she pushed her skirt up so it was in a bunch around her waist, then climbed on top of her, locking their mouths together before reaching down to slip a finger into her. Allison moaned and began rocking her hips again. Ash kissed her neck and nibbled on her ear, but when she took a deep breath she was overwhelmed by the scent of a shampoo similar to Carrie's. She shook her head to banish the image of Carrie smiling up at her.

"What is it?" Allison asked.

Ash thought quickly. "I was just breathing you in."

Allison had a beautiful smile but Ash couldn't stop comparing it to Carrie's. She closed her eyes and inched her way down, parting Allison's legs and going though the motions. The nibbling, the teasing. Gradually she worked herself back into the rhythm of their bodies. Tension built and she allowed herself to get carried away. She couldn't help but smile at her own abilities as she granted the requests for sweet release and felt the shudder of profound pleasure sweep through the body she was holding.

"Wow," Allison exhaled. "You're good."

"Thanks, you're not bad yourself."

"Oh, how can I ever repay you?" the blonde teased.

"I'm sure you'll think of something."

In a heartbeat she was being straddled and any remaining articles of clothing were removed. Two hands and one eager mouth ran seductively over her body. Allison covered her in slow kisses, taking her all in from her earlobes to her fingertips. She certainly had a well-developed sense of timing. She pushed Ash onto her back, stroked her to the edge of orgasm, then withdrew at exactly the right time to keep her from letting go. Ash got a taste of her own medicine as her body cried out each time Allison's expert fingers left her at the last minute. Her pride kept her from begging for only so long, and as she neared orgasm once again she heard herself call out, "That's enough!"

Allison got the message loud and clear, but as she plunged forward, Ash heard Carrie's voice, and while her body went crashing over the edge her mind flashed back to Carrie sitting at the table so close their shoulders brushed up against each other. Carrie smiling, Carrie responding, Carrie snapping, "That's enough!" bringing her and Tess's argument to a close.

Disconcerted, Ash rolled onto her side. She could feel the woman next to her but she couldn't look at her yet. As their breathing slowed, she opened her eyes. Allison was illumined by the mixture of moonlight and streetlamp that shone through the window of the hotel room. Ash thought that if they'd met under different circumstances, she would have seen her again. She might have even made a weekend out of it, but now she knew it was time to go.

"It's okay," Allison whispered. "You can go whenever you want."

"No, I don't need…how did you know?" Ash asked.

"You and I are cut from the same cloth. I don't care for sleepovers much, either." Allison got out of bed and wrapped herself in the hotel bathrobe.

Ash sat up, grabbing her jeans from the foot of the bed and looking around the luxurious hotel room for the first time. "That's refreshing." She laughed nervously. "Will I see you around?"

"No, I'm just here on business."

Ash scanned the room for her jacket, unsure how to handle the frankness about their intentions with each other. In the past the agreement had always been unspoken at best. "Well, thank you for tonight."

"Oh, no, thank you." Allison lifted Ash's jacket from the back of the chair, took a business card from the nightstand, and tucked it into one of the pockets. "If you ever make it to Milwaukee, give me a call." She tossed the jacket to Ash.

Ash slipped it on and met Allison in the middle of the room, pulling her close for one more deep kiss before heading toward the door.

As she turned the handle, Allison said, "Whoever she is, she's a lucky woman."

Ash didn't ask who she was talking about. She was afraid that she already knew the answer.

Ash settled into the driver's seat of her Mustang. The clock on the dashboard showed it was four thirty a.m. There was no use trying to sleep now. She revved the engine and tore out of the parking lot. The evening had turned chilly, but she rolled the window down, hoping the fresh air would clear her mind. She had just enough time to stop by an all-night grocery store before heading over to the quiet neighborhood where Mary and Sharon lived.

The sun wouldn't rise for another hour, but Ash could see streaks of pink creeping slowly across the horizon as she idled in the driveway. Ash knew her best friend would be up at five a.m. even though it was a Sunday and she wouldn't have to be at church for another four hours. Mary's schedule was as predictable as her personality. Right on time, the light flicked on and she pushed past the screen door onto the porch of the picture-perfect starter home.

As Ash bounded up the steps to greet her, Mary quipped, "Thou art up-roused by some distemperature; Or if not so, then here I hit it right, Our Romeo hath not been in bed to-night."

"Fair Juliet, I come bearing doughnuts." Ash gave her best Shakespearean bow.

"How could a lady refuse an offer like that?" Mary plopped down on the porch swing and motioned for Ash to join her. "Didn't things work out with Blondie?"

"Oh, things worked out quite nicely, thank you very much." Ash took a bite of a glazed doughnut and licked the excess sugar icing off her fingers.

"Then what's wrong?"

"Does something have to be wrong for me to come visit my best friend?"

"At five in the morning when we only saw each other a few hours ago? Yes."

"I see how you are."

"Yeah, and?"

"I think I want my doughnut back." Ash reached for the doughnut in Mary's hand, but Mary laughingly pushed her away.

"You're stalling."

"Well, Dr. Freud, I keep having these dreams—"

"Fine." Mary threw up her hands in frustration. "Don't tell me."

A few minutes passed in silence as they rocked the porch

swing back and forth, soaking in the crisp morning air. Ash examined the contrast of her boots on the chipped paint and aging wood of the porch. The pristine white was beginning to peel off, revealing a lower level of gray. She released a heavy sigh. "Your porch needs painting. I could do it next week before it gets too cold."

"You're here to discuss home renovation projects?"

Ash hesitated. "No, I was thinking about something you said earlier. Why wouldn't Carrie go for me?"

Mary gave her an odd look. "Carrie?"

"It's no big deal. I was just wondering."

"I told you, you're just not her type," Mary said softly, as if trying to let her down gently. "You have different goals out of a relationship. She's always looking at the big picture, in every part of her life, and—"

"And I'm just looking for the next lay? Is that it?"

Mary seemed taken aback. "Ashton, why are you so upset about this?"

Ash stood up. She wasn't ready to face the answer to that question. Doing so would force her to delve into feelings she couldn't explain. "It's not important. I think I might just be really tired. I'm going to go get some sleep."

Mary stood up next to her. "I'm worried about you. It's not like you to show up at all hours of the morning mumbling about some woman you just met."

"I'm fine. I'll see you at the cookout?"

"Promise?"

Ash kissed her cheek. "I promise." She stopped briefly in the driveway before getting back into the car. Mary was still standing on the porch watching her go. Ash called, "Hey, who's Judith Butler?"

Mary gave her a questioning look. "She's a feminist scholar. I think she has a new book out. Why?"

"No reason. I'll see you later, okay?"

"I'll be here."

Drowsiness set in as soon as Ash got in the car. She was too exhausted emotionally and physically to dwell on things any more for now. After she got some sleep, maybe she would be thinking clearly again.

CHAPTER FIVE

Ash glanced at her reflection in the glass panes of Mary's front door. She was wearing a nicer pair of jeans and a button-down blue shirt. Her appearance wasn't formal by anyone's standards, but it was as close as she ever came to Sunday best. The five hours of sleep she'd had were enough to force her body back on track. Now if only her mind would do the same. She wasn't afraid to admit that Carrie had gotten her attention. What beautiful woman didn't? What bothered her was that this one was still on her mind. No woman had ever been worth the time and effort of thinking about after they'd parted ways, and certainly no one warranted a second meeting if the first didn't work out. What was so special about Carrie Fletcher? Ash couldn't believe she was willing to endure another youth center function just to see her. Whatever it was, Ash intended to find out.

"Hello," she called as she stepped inside Mary's house.

A chorus of greetings arose from the living room.

Mary gave her a hug and took her coat. "Are you feeling better?"

"Yeah, I'm fine." Ash followed her toward the other guests.

"I tried to call you when we got home from church this morning, but your phone was off the hook."

"Sorry, I needed to sleep."

"What's the matter?" Michael asked, butting into their conversation. "You're not sick, are you?"

"No, I was just getting some rest."

"What she means is she had a busy night, much too busy for sleep, I'm sure." Tess got in her first dig.

"And we're off." Ash tried to laugh. "Not even a hello before you start in on me, Tess?"

"Hello. Did you miss me?" Tess's coy smile suggested that despite last night's dismissal she was ready to try again.

"For God's sake, let the woman get through the door before you start hammering her with the twenty questions," Sharon bellowed. She was a voluptuous woman with a warm smile and hearty laugh. Slapping Ash on the back, she said, "Grab a beer and come help me with the grill."

Thankful for the rescue, Ash shook her hand and made a beeline for the refrigerator. As she rounded the corner to the kitchen, she was confronted with the image of Carrie standing at the sink, talking to Annie, who was perched on the counter. Ash stopped dead in her tracks and watched Carrie nod at the mumbled ramblings of the child. She bit her nail, looking increasingly nervous as Annie repeated herself with more force.

"I'm sorry, I just don't know what you want."

"Hey hey mil peas," Annie said, waving her tiny hand.

Carrie continued to chew on her fingernail, and Ash smiled at how cute she was when she wasn't playing the poised professor. She had the sudden urge to draw her into her arms and hold her close. Instead, she opened the fridge door and extracted one of the sippy-cups stored inside. "One hey hey mil coming right up. That's a chocolate milk, for those of you who don't speak toddler."

Carrie released a relieved sigh. "You understand her. I'm impressed."

"We're good buddies." Ash reached over to tickle Annie for emphasis.

The toddler giggled and pushed her hand away.

Carrie smiled. "She really likes you."

"She's easy to impress. All you need to win her over is a few cookies." To make her point she passed a cookie to Carrie, who bestowed it on Annie with delight.

"Great, now there's two of you spoiling her." Mary entered the room, lifted Annie into her arms, and departed with a pointed look at each of them.

Carrie clutched Ash's arm as they both burst out laughing. "You got me in trouble."

"Ah, Mary will get over it, but now Annie will love you forever." Ash loved to hear Carrie laugh, and the feel of her hand was almost enough to make her melt.

"I thought you said you weren't comfortable with kids."

"No, I said I wasn't good with teenagers. Kids are easy. Kids I like."

"Do you want to have any of your own?"

Ash stared down at the hand still resting unnervingly on her bicep. Without thinking, she blurted, "God, who in their right mind would ever have a kid with me?"

Carrie seemed taken aback by the flippant tone of her statement and immediately broke the contact between them.

Ash was startled to feel incredibly empty from the withdrawal. Scrambling to regain the connection, she said, "I mean, I guess I've never really thought about having kids before. What about you?"

"I don't know." Carrie sounded interested and Ash could tell she'd relaxed again. "I like the idea of helping to shape the next generation, making it better than the one that came before. That probably sounds silly, though, doesn't it?"

"Not at all. When you put it like that, it sounds pretty nice," Ash answered honestly. This was certainly not the type of conversation she was used to having but somehow, when she looked into Carrie's deep blue eyes, the subject didn't feel as threatening.

"Well, it's a moot point right now anyway. I've got way too much invested in work to even think about starting a relationship, much less build the type of home life I'd want to bring a child into."

"For what it's worth, I think you would make a great parent," Ash said.

Slowly the conversation stopped, and Ash was at a loss for words. She struggled to think of something charming but couldn't stop staring at Carrie.

"Yes?"

"You look nice," she blurted out.

Nice? Ash cursed herself. Carrie looked better than nice. She was wearing cream-colored slacks and a black blouse with a neck that was cut just low enough to make Ash's mind wander where it shouldn't.

"Thanks," Carrie responded shyly, seeming both pleased and slightly embarrassed with the compliment. "I should go see if Amy needs any help setting up the table."

"Yeah," Ash said, reluctant for the moment to end. "I'd better give Sharon a hand."

Carrie nodded and headed into the other room. Once again all Ash could do was watch her go.

Mary and Sharon's back yard was exactly what anyone would expect to find from looking at the front of the house. A large oak tree shaded a swing set Ash had helped Sharon assemble for Annie's first birthday. On the other side of the yard vegetables grew in three or four rows. Mary tended these more as a hobby than anything else, but a few of the tomato plants still looked like they might produce. Closer to the house, just beyond the sliding doors, was a small wooden picnic table and the grill.

Ash found Sharon there, flipping burgers. "How's it going?" she asked, inspecting the burgers appreciatively. She hadn't eaten much over the past twenty-four hours and the smell made her mouth water.

"Pretty good. This batch is about done."

"You want me to get some hot dogs out?"

"Sure." Sharon indicated a package on the nearest picnic table.

After Ash added these to the grill, she stood in silence for a moment, staring blankly at the meat cooking over the glowing coals.

"Long night?" Sharon finally asked, moving some of the burgers onto a platter.

"You could say that."

"What did you think of the youth center?"

Ash rolled her eyes, not really sure how to handle that question diplomatically.

"That good, huh?"

"It had its moments."

"You don't have to sugarcoat it for me," Sharon said. "The whole center thing isn't my cup of tea either. I'd rather baby-sit one kid than a whole room full of them."

Ash wasn't surprised by Sharon's views. Mary was the one who wanted a family, something Ash couldn't understand, much less provide, back when they were seeing each other. But Sharon had been able and willing, and Ash respected that. She hadn't protested when Mary started dating her. She'd understood that it was time for both of them to move on with the lives they wanted. The decision had worked out well for Mary, and Ash was happy about that, but every now and then she had the sense that she'd let Mary down.

"Mary seems to think the center is important," Ash said, toeing the politically correct line. "Kids need a safe place to go just in case the real world gets complicated."

"Well, I think they need good role models," Sharon conceded. "I'm just glad that other people, like Mary and Carrie, enjoy being that for them."

"Amen to that." Ash turned the hot dogs.

"At least the night wasn't a total waste for you. Mary said you found yourself some after-hours entertainment."

Ash grinned. "Is that how she put it?"

"No, I think she said you just glanced at some blonde and her clothes fell off."

Ash shook her head, but was secretly pleased at the assessment of her charisma. "Your wife has a flair for the dramatic. It took me a good hour and a half to get Blondie's clothes to fall off."

Sharon shook her head. "I don't know how you do it."

"Sure you do. You were the same way before you met Mary."

"I guess." Sharon ran her hand through her chin-length black hair. She was still attractive despite the air of domesticity she had acquired over the years. "It's just hard to imagine doing it now."

"Why?" Ash was genuinely interested. She'd never understood how someone could not want to fall into bed with a beautiful woman.

"I don't know. I guess I just grew out of it."

"Grew out of what? Sex?"

"Good God, no. I wasn't tired of the sex. I got tired of the instability. I mean, I would have great sex and then that would be it. No follow-up, no next time. Afterward there was nothing, you know?"

Ash nodded. "Sounds good to me."

"Yeah, most of the time, until…" Sharon paused, thoughtfully choosing her words. "Until you meet someone you want to be there in the morning and they aren't."

"So you chose to settle down because you wanted a second date?"

Sharon regarded her with a mixture of amusement and patience. "When I met Mary, it wasn't so much that I wanted a second date so much as I was terrified I wouldn't get one."

Ash looked down at her shoes. She didn't know what to say to that. Yesterday she would have scoffed at the idea that any woman was worth forgoing all others for, but she was still shaken up by her conversation in the kitchen with Carrie.

"It wasn't even really a conscious choice," Sharon said. "I just knew I wanted her more than I'd ever want anyone else. Then next thing I knew, I had a wife, a baby, and a picket fence." She sounded awfully content with how her life had turned out.

Ash couldn't help but wonder if that was what Carrie had been talking about when she mentioned a woman worth building a family with.

"Don't you ever miss the thrill of the chase?" she asked Sharon.

"Occasionally I think about it, but then I look at Annie and Mary, and I realize I'm not missing a thing."

Ash couldn't decide whether she found this answer disturbing or comforting. The events of the past twenty-four hours had her second-guessing herself, and she didn't like the feeling. "I think the hot dogs are done," Sharon finally said, bringing Ash back to the situation at hand. "Think we should head back into the three-ring circus that's taken over my house?"

"I guess if we don't go in soon, they'll probably send a search party," Ash responded.

"Come on," Sharon said as they headed inside. "If we present a unified front, we might be able to get some football on TV."

The crowd gathered around the food laid out along the kitchen counter and tables. A jumble of hands filled red plastic plates with burgers and dogs, corn on the cob, and various other staples of a Midwest cookout. Ash made her way through the line, taking at least one helping of everything. With the weather already turning cooler, this would probably be her last cookout for a good five or six months.

She wandered through the house to the living room, where most of the teens were eating in front of the TV. Carrie was nowhere to be seen, so Ash sat on the couch, balancing her plate on her knees. She was just shoveling a spoonful of Mary's famous bacon-baked-beans into her mouth when she felt someone plop down next to her. She didn't have to even look up to know that the thigh rubbing against hers was Tess's.

Ash rolled her eyes at the blatant invasion of her personal space, but she didn't want to let the girl get a rise out of her. Tess was wearing skintight jeans and an equally snug turtleneck. She was a little overdressed for a cookout, but Ash realized the look was probably intentional. With a polite smile, she shifted so there was minimal contact between their bodies.

"So," Tess said coyly. "What did you do last night?"

"Sorry, kiddo." Ash chose a patronizing tone. "You have to reach puberty before I can tell you stories like that."

Tess acted if the remark hadn't been made. "Maybe we could share little black books sometime."

"I'm sure the girls at your middle school would enjoy that kind of game, but you're out of your league with me."

"Actually I'm in high school, but if you like 'em young I'm sure I could pretend."

"Wow, you really do live in a fantasy world, don't you?" Ash returned her attention to her food.

Tess didn't accept the dismissal. "We all have fantasies. I'll tell you mine if you tell me yours."

Ash sighed heavily. She couldn't figure out why Tess kept trying to drag her into these types of discussions when she made her disapproval obvious. She glanced around, hoping none of the adults had tuned in to the conversation. Wondering whether she should simply get up and leave the room, she said, "Go bug someone else."

"Why? I'm not your type?"

"How 'bout those Bears?" Ash said pleasantly. "They're off to a great start this year."

But Tess was determined to get under her skin. "You like

older women, then? Someone more settled, more respectable? Someone, like, I don't know, maybe a professor?"

Ash felt a cold chill run down her spine. "Watch it, kid."

"You dated Mary, she teaches elementary. Then on to Amy, she's got high school covered…"

Ash gritted her teeth, fighting the urge to retort in kind. Normally she wouldn't let a kid bug her so much, but Tess seemed to know which buttons to push. Determined not to allow the girl to get her riled up, she gave her a bored look and got to her feet.

"Don't get all bent out of shape," Tess called as she walked away. "I don't blame you for being hot for teacher."

Ash spun around quickly, feeling her temper slipping out of control but unable to do anything about it. Everyone in the room had fallen silent, staring expectantly. "You need to learn to show some respect for the women in your life," she said angrily. "Until you do, stay out of my way." With that she grabbed her coat off the rack and shut the door too hard on her way out.

Taking deep breaths of the cool autumn air, she sat on the porch swing and tried to figure out why Tess hit such a nerve with her and why the mere mention of Carrie was enough to make her snap. Wasn't Tess just some punk teenager? Wasn't Carrie perfectly capable of defending her own honor? Wasn't she the one who just wanted to live and let live? What happened to things being uncomplicated? What happened to the lovely Ritas of the world? Rita. Was that really just three days ago? It seemed so much further away than that. She wondered what had changed so drastically since Thursday night.

Behind her, the front door opened and she hung her head, expecting Mary to step out and scold her for failing to control her temper. But the sweet smell of Carrie's shampoo tickled her senses as Carrie took the seat next to her on the swing. They sat quietly for a few seconds, rocking gently back and forth, Ash trying to keep her head from spinning. She couldn't believe this woman was so intoxicating to her. Having her so close made Ash's stomach clench with nerves and some other feeling she wasn't used to. She wished she could come up with a smart observation, but her usual throwaway lines eluded her.

"I'm sorry," Carrie finally said.

"*You're* sorry?" Ash fought not to melt into those deep blue eyes. "You have nothing to be sorry for."

"I'm not sure exactly what happened in there, but I've known Tess for a long time, so I've got a pretty good idea. She has quite the talent for knowing how to get to people."

"Yes, she does, but that doesn't justify me blowing my top."

"Ash, I know we don't know each other well." Ash's heart skipped a beat as she heard her name roll off Carrie's tongue. "But would you consider doing me a favor?"

"Just name it." She kicked herself for sounding too eager, but at that moment she would have done anything to get Carrie to smile at her again. She couldn't figure out why that smile sent her over the edge, but she was quickly becoming addicted to Dr. Carrie Fletcher. There was no point denying it.

"Will you promise me you won't give up on Tess?"

"Give up? I don't mean to sound rude, but I don't know what there is to give up on." Ash felt her will buckle at the hint of sadness on Carrie's face.

Carrie paused, oddly affected by the look in Ash's eyes. For some reason, she felt the need to make Ash see the potential she saw in Tess. "She hasn't always been like this. She used to be a happy kid. She's just been knocked around so much that she's becoming jaded."

"Yeah?" Ash seemed interested. "How long have you known her?"

"A little over five years. I had just started working at the university, bought my first house, and when I showed up to move in, Tess was climbing the tree in my front yard." Carrie smiled at the memory. She would give anything to see a glimpse of that happy kid again. "She just invited herself in and seemed to have a comment for everything I unpacked."

"That sounds like Tess."

"She was smart and wild, and I realized very quickly that her mother hated both of those things about her." Carrie tried to read Ash's expression. Was any of this registering? Mary had said that Ash was a lot like Tess when she was a teenager: strong willed, rebellious. Would she be able to draw that link herself, or was the possibility of a connection just wishful thinking?

"So you took her in?" Ash asked.

"I tried to help as much as I could. That's why I've been bringing her to the center for the past two years, but her mother isn't very accommodating."

"Tess seems to be able to stand up for herself pretty well."

"I know she can come on pretty strong, but she's still just a teenager. She shouldn't have to go through everything on her own. She deserves to be cared for. She deserves to have people who can show her a life where she can be herself without having to fight all the time."

Can you be one of those people, Ash? Carrie wondered silently. She reasoned that while Tess was used to getting reactions out of people, it was rare that anyone was able to truly go toe-to-toe with her the way Ash did. That wasn't necessarily a positive, but it was something, and at this point anything was better than nothing.

"I'm really not sure what I can do to help," Ash said. "But if you want me to, I'll try to keep my mind open."

"Thanks." Carrie smiled. "That's all I ask."

She wasn't sure exactly what she expected, she just knew she had to keep trying. Somewhere deep down was the Tess she remembered, a kid untouched by the cynicism and bitterness Carrie now saw in her. She still held out hope that Tess could be that kid again. In the meantime, Carrie didn't want her alienating everyone who could help her.

❖

The rest of the afternoon went without incident. As the after-lunch lethargy set in, people sprawled out in various places around the house to watch TV or just talk to one another. Ash spent most of her time lying on the couch pretending to be engrossed in a football game. Occasionally she and Sharon would comment on a particularly good or bad play, but for the most part Ash was left to her thoughts. She must have dozed off awhile because she didn't notice people leaving.

When she finally looked around, it was almost five p.m. and she, Carrie, and Tess were the only visitors left. Tess lay on the floor idly stacking blocks into towers with Annie, and Carrie and Mary were wiping down tables and counter tops. Sharon was asleep in the recliner across the room.

Ash sat up and stretched her legs before standing up. She was heading for the kitchen, but felt a tug on the bottom of her pant leg. She looked down to see Annie pointing at the block tower she and Tess had built.

Ash smiled and crouched between the girls. "That is great, Annie. Did you make it?"

The child smiled and nodded vigorously. As an afterthought, she pointed to Tess as if to say, *She helped, too.*

Ash laughed. "Well, then, you both did a good job."

"Really, it was nothing." Tess feigned a regal air. "I'd really just like to thank all the little people that helped me on the way up."

"Did you hear that, Annie? She called you a little person," Ash teased. "You're a big girl, aren't you? How big are you?"

Annie, taking her cue to perform, stood up on her tiptoes and stretched her arms up as high as she could get them.

"Oh yeah, she's so big!" Ash finished the routine. With a wink to Tess, she added, "See, she's a big girl."

Tess gave both of them a genuine smile, the first Ash had seen out of her, and said, "Okay, big girl, ready to knock it down?"

That was all the invitation Annie needed. She swung her hand right to the base of the tower and squealed with delight as it came crashing to the floor. Ash and Tess laughed, and so did Carrie. Ash hadn't seen her come around the corner from the kitchen to the living room carrying a stack of folding chairs.

"Here, let me help with those." Ash jumped up.

"I've got these," Carrie answered, "but you can get the rest of them from the kitchen if you want to help. Mary said they go in the attic closet."

"Sure, I wanted to show you around up there before you left anyway."

"Great." Carrie smiled.

"Great," Ash echoed, shaking her head at how silly she sounded.

By the time she made it to the top of the attic stairs, Carrie had already stacked her chairs in the closet. Ash propped the remaining few against the wall and walked over to her. "It's not a masterpiece or anything, but it was pretty rough up here when I started."

She ran her fingers over the soft baby blue windowsill. The room was small, but it was light and airy, decorated in whites and blues and yellows. The ceilings slanted gently toward the floor, but there was a window set back into a dormer on each of its four sides, creating the illusion of having more space.

"It's beautiful," Carrie said, taking in the entire room.

"The floorboards are the originals. I just refinished them," Ash said. "There were big nails coming through the ceiling, so I put up some insulation and drywalled it. Then I found the wood trim that matched the floor."

"I can't believe you did all this."

"Well, when Mary was pregnant with Annie, she and Sharon turned her old studio into the nursery." Ash stepped closer to Carrie. "I thought Mary would need a space that she could have to herself, to paint or write or whatever."

"A room of one's own," Carrie said softly.

"Yeah, something like that."

Ash took the final step, closing the distance between them. She gazed directly into those deep blue eyes and couldn't help but feel like she could see straight into Carrie's soul. They stood there face-to-face, suspended for an eternity, before Ash lowered her head slightly, breathing in Carrie's sweet scent. But just before their lips met, Carrie turned away and crossed hastily to the bookcases on the other side of the room.

Ash wasn't sure what had happened, but the connection between them was broken.

"And these bookshelves, did you make them, too?" Carrie asked with just the slightest hint of shakiness.

"Um, yeah." Ash swallowed hard, her head spinning wildly. She struggled to regain her composure. "They were harder than I expected. The floors are uneven, so I had to adjust the shelves to keep them from being slanted, but you know, Mary's a teacher, so she has a lot of books and not enough space for all of them."

"I know the feeling." Carrie sighed. "I would love to have something like this for my office."

"I could take a look sometime. Maybe I could build you some shelves."

"Oh, no." Carrie looked flushed. "I mean, I couldn't ask you to do that."

"Why? Are the floors uneven in there, too?" Ash tried to joke.

Carrie laughed nervously. "No, it's just that I know you must be busy."

"Actually," Ash ran her hand through her hair, trying to recall the jobs she had lined up, "I'm busy tomorrow, but I'm completely open Tuesday and Wednesday."

"I don't know." Carrie looked uneasy.

"It wouldn't hurt for me to just come look and see if I can do anything." Ash wondered for a split second if she was pushing too hard, but she knew she had to see Carrie again and she couldn't wait until next Saturday at the center. Was she really thinking of going back to that youth center?

"I guess it wouldn't hurt for you to come by on Tuesday afternoon," Carrie said.

Ash tried to keep the silly grin on her face to a minimum. "How about one?"

"That would be fine." Carrie smiled slightly. "I'm in Stetson Hall, office two-sixteen J. Do you know your way around the campus?"

"I think I can find it."

"Okay, then, one o'clock Tuesday afternoon."

"Sounds great." Ash kicked herself for not being more charming.

"All right, then. I'd better get Tess home."

"I'll put the rest of the chairs away."

"See you Tuesday."

"Yes, see you then."

As Carrie headed back down the stairs, Ash wasn't sure whether to be disappointed that she didn't get the kiss that had seemed so imminent or overjoyed that she was going to see her again in less than forty-eight hours.

"Carrie left awfully quickly." Mary stood at the kitchen sink, up to her elbows in soap suds. Annie was next to her in a high chair, happily tapping the food tray with a wooden spoon.

Ash picked up a dish rag and began absentmindedly drying the plates Mary handed to her. She still wasn't sure what had happened upstairs. She and Carrie had been so close, she'd been certain they were both feeling the same attraction to one another. So what went wrong?

"What did you do to her?" Mary demanded, obviously reading the frustration on her face.

"Nothing. I might be building her some bookshelves for her office. We were in the attic. She likes the work I did for you."

Mary eyed her suspiciously. "And?"

"Nothing happened. I mean, I almost kissed her. We were inches away but we didn't."

"You *almost* kissed her and now you *might* be building her a bookcase?" Mary raised her eyebrows.

"I know. I mean I don't know. Really, she's confusing me."

"What do you want with her?" Mary asked bluntly.

"I don't know."

"I do. You want to," Mary covered Annie's ears and said in an exaggerated whisper, "have sex with her."

Ash let the wet plate she was holding slip from her hand and it crashed to the floor. "Shit," she muttered, sending Annie into a fit of giggles.

"Ash!" Mary scolded.

"Sorry." She stooped to pick up the pieces of the plate she'd dropped, thankful Mary wouldn't see her blushing.

"She's got you all wound up." Mary chuckled softly. "Are you sure it's just sex you're after this time?"

"Yes. I mean no. Well, that's certainly part of it." Ash tried to laugh off the seriousness in her friend's voice.

"And then what? Add her to your long list of conquered women, move on to the next challenge?" Mary asked matter-of-factly.

"It's not like that." She stood up and dumped the shards of ceramic in the trash while Mary continued washing dishes.

"It's not? How is it different this time?" Mary listed possible alternatives to a one-night stand like she was checking off a grocery list. "You want a relationship? You want to date her?"

"Come on, dating is for kids. I haven't been on a date since… well, since you."

Mary's face went pink, and her voice softened. "Carrie isn't like the hundreds of women you've been with in the past ten years. For a start, she's not going to let you hurt her."

"You think I want to hurt her?" Ash was stung by the idea. Hurting Carrie was the last thing she intended.

"No, and that's why I'm asking you to stop and think before you act this time." Mary put her arm around Ash's shoulder. "You know I love you. I just want you to be careful with Carrie. She deserves that, and so do you."

"I'm not sure I know how to do things like that," Ash confessed.

"Like what?" Mary asked.

Ash shrugged.

Mary tossed the sponge at her unexpectedly, splashing water across her shirt.

"Hey," Ash laughed, tossing it back at her.

Mary quickly grabbed the spray handle on the sink and pointed it at Ash as though prepared to squirt her at any second. "Stop avoiding me, or you'll get drenched," she warned. "What is it that you're so afraid of?"

Ash felt her cheeks getting even warmer. "The whole handholding, trips to the movies, or dinner, or whatever two people supposedly do before they get to doing what it is they really want to do with each other. I'm not good at it."

Mary put down her water weapon. "It's been a while, but I remember a time when you did all those things, and I think deep down you do, too."

All Ash could do was nod. She wondered for the first time in years if she was even capable of having a real relationship. She liked sex, and she was good at it. She'd grown so accustomed to focusing on the physical that she no longer even thought about any other level of connection. She had friends, and she had sex, and the two hadn't gone together for a long time. Even if she wanted them to, she wasn't sure if she could make that happen.

"I should get going," she said. "I have to teach the League of Women Voters how to change a flat tire tomorrow."

Mary laughed. "Well, far be it from me to get in the way of the League of Women Voters. Just be careful."

"They're a bunch of old ladies with car jacks. I think I'll be okay."

"That wasn't what I was talking about."

"No." Ash smiled. "I didn't think it was."

She kissed Annie on the forehead and Mary on the cheek before grabbing her coat and stepping out into the increasingly cold autumn evening.

CHAPTER SIX

Yes, like that. Crank it up enough to take some of the pressure off the rim," Ash told the group of retired women that made up the local chapter of the League of Women Voters. "Be careful not to jack it up all the way off the ground yet. You don't want the tire spinning while you're taking off the lug nuts."

The women watched intently as she helped one of their members turn the lever on the jack that was supporting her 1995 Buick LeSabre.

"Okay, now we need to remove the lug nuts, so who's got the lug wrench?" Several of the women looked at the tools in their hands. "It looks like a plus sign." Ash crossed her forearms to show the shape of the tool.

"I've got it!" Betty Ryan, a petite woman who looked to be about sixty, waved the wrench.

"Great, bring it up here." Ash put her arm around Betty's shoulder. "Are you ready to tackle these lug nuts?"

"You better believe it. Just let me at 'em."

Ash laughed. "Now put the wrench on one of them and turn it to the left."

"Lefty, loosey," Betty intoned.

She was able to remove three of the lug nuts on her own before running into trouble on the fourth. Ash got behind her, so they were grasping the wrench in unison. With their combined strength the lug nut spun right off.

"There you go," Ash said. "It just needed a bit of prodding."

"Thank you, Ms. Clarke, but next time, before you get so fresh with me, I do think you should at least buy me a drink." Betty chuckled, sending the rest of the women into titters.

Ash was somewhat taken aback by the reference to her sexual orientation, but couldn't help but chuckle when Betty wiggled her eyebrows in an exaggerated come-hither look. "Betty, my dear, I would buy you a drink anytime."

Betty blushed. "Oh, you scoundrel." She shook the lug wrench at her.

Palms up in mock surrender, Ash said, "All right, you win. Now put that thing where it should be."

After the demonstration was finished, the women all headed into Betty's house. Ash intended to stay only long enough to wash her hands, but as she was getting ready to slip away, Betty caught her by the arm.

"Oh no, you don't. You're not getting away that easily. You haven't even had our punch and brownies."

"I really don't want to impose."

"Nonsense. You sit down, and I'll get you a drink."

Before Ash could argue, she was next to Betty on the couch with a drink in her hand. She took a sip of what looked like fruit punch. The red liquid hit first her tongue and then her throat, burning the entire way down. As the acrid fumes rose through her nose, tears stung her eyes and she stood up, coughing and sputtering. "Jesus! What's in there?" she croaked.

"Hey, hey, watch your damn language." Betty tsked before turning to the other ladies. "Looks like we've got a lightweight on our hands, girls."

Ash sniffed tentatively at the drink. "I was expecting Kool-Aid."

The women laughed.

"No, honey, this isn't a day care, and that isn't Kool-Aid," Betty said. "That, my dear, is Sill's famous artillery punch. It's a divine combination of Benedictine, brandy, red wine, dark rum, and whiskey, with some fruit juices thrown in for good measure."

"You drink this stuff in the middle of the day?" Ash examined the glass in her hand, amazed that any of her students could walk in a straight line after a glass of this so-called punch.

"It's always five o'clock somewhere," Betty answered casually.

"Any more surprises for me, Betty? Are the brownies filled with hash?"

"Oh, my good heavens no. Not with all the blood work I get at checkups these days. I'd never get away with it."

Ash couldn't tell if she was being sarcastic or not. "Really, Betty, what's this about your daughter?"

"Well, I'm glad you asked," Betty said, pulling a picture out of her purse and handing it to Ash. "That's my daughter, Cheryl."

"She's lovely," Ash answered, not really understanding why she was looking at the picture of the altogether nondescript, thirtysomething Cheryl.

"I thought you'd notice. She'll be in town over Thanksgiving weekend, and I know she'd love to meet you."

The warning bells began to go off in Ash's head. "Betty, are you suggesting I take your daughter out on a date?"

"Exactly." Betty beamed. "She goes to graduate school in Boston, but I'd really like her to come back home, find a nice girl, and settle down."

"This is a first."

"Why?"

"Usually mothers want nothing more than the big bad butch to stay far away from their daughters." Ash laughed.

"Oh pshaw, child. I started college in 1961. I'm the original feminist, and don't you forget it. You women today think you're so liberal with your sexual politics, but you weren't even thought of when I was marching along with women like Betty Friedan."

"I'm sorry, Betty. I obviously misread you."

"Well, my kids are all grown up now, and I think Cheryl would only consider moving back if she met someone here she could identify with." Betty's tone had gone soft again.

"I would love to help you." Ash smiled, thinking about Betty getting so fired up over feminism. "But really, I don't think it would work out."

"Why not? You're single, aren't you?"

"Yes, but I guess you could say I have my eye on someone."

"What are you waiting for?" Betty slapped her knee. "A hot piece of work like you. I'm sure this woman would love a shot at you."

Ash couldn't help but find the conversation a little odd, but Betty's bluntness was endearing. "I'll try to keep that in mind when I see her tomorrow."

"You do that." Betty paused for a moment before asking, "Do you have any friends you could introduce Cheryl to?"

"I'm not sure your daughter would appreciate you butting into her love life, but I'll keep her in mind if I run into anyone."

"Ah, it's a mother's job to butt in. I'll never give up on getting her back home and back in the church."

"The church?" Ash asked skeptically. "What church?"

"The Catholic church, dear."

"Betty, you're full of contradictions. You spend ten minutes telling me you're as liberal as they come, but you're also a practicing Catholic?"

"The two aren't contradictions, just people's stereotypes of them. You of all people should know better than to buy into stereotypes."

"Touché, but I was raised in the Catholic church. Based on the teachings of my family's priest, the stereotypes of the Catholic church ring pretty true, at least in the realm of homophobia."

"Well, despite what that priest may think, he is not God, and therefore he does not get to dictate my faith," Betty said.

"Oh? I didn't know you could make your own rules in the Catholic church."

"I didn't make the rules about loving God and loving my neighbor. I just know that my life would have been much worse without some kind of heavenly grace."

"Well, that I can understand," Ash said, glad for the chance to wrap the discussion up amicably.

She left the house with Betty's phone number in her wallet and plans to meet her for lunch next week. The League of Women Voters had been an unusual but pleasant surprise, to say the least. She couldn't help but notice that her strange weekend seemed to have seeped into her week as well.

Ash took a detour on the way home in order to pass by the university. It was dusk as she drove slowly down the narrow streets lined on either side by picturesque, ivy-clad brick buildings. Students congested the sidewalks, walking from place to place with books in hand. Ash had been on campus only a few times and didn't know her way around, but she liked the feel of the place, so she took several trips around the main section with her windows rolled down, taking in the feel of the crisp autumn air and the sight of the trees with their leaves just beginning to show hints of red and orange. On her third time down the shaded lane she noticed a sign outside one of buildings. Stetson Hall.

Ash caught herself smiling at the thought of Carrie walking down the stairs in front of the large glass doors to meet her. For a minute she could almost understand what Sharon had been talking about on Sunday, and that scared her. She slowed the Mustang, looking at the windows lit up from inside, wondering if Carrie was behind one of them. She suddenly had the urge to go find 216J and see if she was there, but then what would she do? This was new territory for her and she didn't know if she cared for the feelings she was having.

When the person behind her tapped his horn, she started out

of her daydreams. The urge to loop back around for another look almost overtook her, but she decided it was better not to know if Carrie was still in her office. She'd see her tomorrow and, if their past encounters were any indication of things to come, that was likely to be more than she could handle.

Carrie put down the stack of student papers she'd been perusing. She didn't really grade them per se, she just used them as an opportunity to see how the students were handling the course material. She knew she could make life easy on herself by giving multiple-choice quizzes like many of her colleagues, but she never saw the use in having students memorize mundane facts or vocabulary. She wanted to see how their minds functioned, and whether they were able to relate to the material on a meaningful level. Reading the text wasn't enough. Carrie wanted them to grapple with the subject, and they couldn't do that if they were just preparing for a fill-in-the-blank assignment. Still, that meant she spent most of her evenings reading personal reflections on Feminism 101 instead of doing something more fun or enlightening.

She glanced at the clock and realized she'd been sitting at the cramped desk in her home office for several hours. No wonder the muscles in her neck and shoulders felt all knotted up. It was late and she had a morning class, but she knew she wouldn't be able to sleep with all the tension in her back, so she headed across the hallway to run a bath. The water was warm, the way she liked it, and the tub was deep and long enough for her to sink into it completely. The bathroom was a big reason why she had bought this house in the first place. It had recently been remodeled with oak cabinets, dark tiled floors, and new plumbing that provided plenty of water pressure for the bath and shower. This room had become her sanctuary.

Carrie felt herself relax as soon as she stepped into the

tub and slid beneath the water. She knew she should probably go over her information for a conference call with the dean of Arts and Sciences tomorrow, but she couldn't bear to look at the depressing statistics again. She didn't need an accountant to tell her that the women's studies enrollment was up forty-eight percent in the past four years, and new faculty appointments were down by twelve. She also knew that no matter how convincing the numbers were, her new budget was likely to be significantly smaller than she recommended. Dean Phillips was never going to pull money away from a male-dominated department like geology or physics.

It was maddening to see her department and her students shortchanged year after year, and she fought as hard as she could to get them a proper allotment of resources, but there was only so much she could do. She was up for tenure next year and the dean never failed to remind her that her job was anything but secure, and insubordination was not a good way to win over the tenure committee. Carrie couldn't meet her goals while constantly worrying if she'd have a job the following year, so she bit her tongue and played the game, at least most of the time.

Just thinking about the politics was enough to cause the tension to creep back into her body. She ran her hand across her shoulders and down her chest, massaging the muscles as she went. *Think about something more pleasant or you'll never be able to relax.* For some reason a vision of Ash filled her mind. They'd been so close in the attic, Carrie had almost given in to her impulses. Something about Ash made her react in ways she never had before. It was like her body was acting on its own accord. She had always been levelheaded and restrained, but for some reason all of that seemed to disappear when Ash got too close.

Her other relationships had been logical, not that there were many. In college she'd dated another women's studies major. They shared an intense passion for the new ideas they were being exposed to. Then in grad school she'd lived with a philosophy student. They had spent several years together working through the rigors of academic initiation. The conversation was easy and stimulating, but the physical aspects had been more awkward and therefore less of a priority. While neither relationship was particularly exciting, both had been satisfying, and Carrie had always prided herself on not losing her mind or rearranging her priorities simply because she found someone attractive. She had goals and she always put her career first.

Yet something about Ash was different. Carrie was surprised to sense a vulnerability to her, just below the surface. When she let her guard down she could be sweet and sensitive. The cocky public image she presented in a crowd seemed to vanish when they were alone, and Carrie thought she was seeing a completely different person. When Ash had leaned so close in Mary's attic, with that look of raw passion in her eyes, Carrie had completely forgotten about her reputation, her academic credibility, and her career goals. All she knew was the feel of Ash's breath on her skin and the heat radiating from her own body. It had taken all of her resolve to turn away, and not a moment too soon. If she'd let their lips touch, she had no idea if she would have been able to regain her composure. She got goose bumps even now when she thought about what might have happened.

She climbed out of the tub and dried off, firmly reminding herself that she didn't need to dwell on what-ifs. She was less than a year away from tenure, and no distraction was worth risking her future for. Still, she couldn't help but sneak a glance in the mirror before wrapping herself in a robe. She was lean, and while not as fit as she would like, her body was firm. She had never considered herself attractive; in fact, she rarely thought about herself in physical terms at all. But she had to admit she was holding up pretty well for a woman in her early thirties.

She blushed suddenly and closed the robe, embarrassed that she was sizing herself up in the mirror like a silly schoolgirl. It didn't matter what she looked like. She wasn't going to get involved with anyone, much less someone with a reputation like Ashton Clarke's. They had absolutely nothing in common, nothing to build a stable relationship on. Not that Ash was one to build stable relationships. Even Mary didn't deny that her best friend was a one-night stand waiting to happen. Physical reactions aside, Ash was a dangerous diversion, one Carrie couldn't afford. No matter how the woman made her feel, she needed to put her physical responses in perspective and stay focused. She hadn't worked this hard to place her future at risk.

CHAPTER SEVEN

Two-sixteen J, two-sixteen J," Ash mumbled to herself as she walked up the stairs inside Stetson Hall.

She had forced herself to drive around the block for half an hour so she wouldn't be too early. She didn't want anyone guessing that she'd been waiting desperately for this moment ever since Carrie left on Sunday. She tried to amble casually down the long hall as she scanned the numbers on each door. The walls were covered in flyers advertising everything from tutoring groups to parties, and students crowded the corridors, either milling about or hurrying to classes. She felt out of place. She obviously wasn't a student, with her tool belt slung over her shoulder rather than the backpacks or briefcases sported by most of the people in the building.

At twenty-eight, Ash was only about five years older than the upperclassmen sitting in the various classrooms she passed, but she felt worlds away. The thought of sitting in one of the long rows of desks for hours on end while someone droned on at an overhead projector was beyond her comprehension. Then she thought of Carrie and couldn't contain a grin. Maybe she would be able to focus on what a professor was saying if they all looked like the woman she was here to see.

Carrie's office was at the very end of a narrow offshoot of

the main hall. Ash took a deep breath and knocked on the door, entering when she heard, "Come in."

Carrie sat at her desk, her silhouette framed by the afternoon sun shining through the blinds behind her. She gave Ash a tired smile and rolled her eyes in the direction of the phone she held a few inches from her ear.

"You can hardly expect us to keep functioning at this level for much longer," Carrie said.

Ash waited in the doorway, shifting her weight awkwardly from one foot to the other, wondering if she should step back outside. Carrie's voice was strained, like she was fighting to sound polite.

"I'm not accusing anyone of anything, Gary. A majority of your students and entry-level professionals are women, but the administration is made up solely of men. If hiring trends don't change soon, it won't be long before this campus will look suspiciously like a harem."

Carrie winced as the voice on the other end of the line got louder. Ash couldn't make out exactly what was being said.

"No, I didn't mean to imply any such thing." Carrie gave a sharp intake of breath and bit at her nail. "No. Thank you very much for your time, Dean Phillips."

With that, she hung up and ran her hand through her curls, stopping to massage the base of her neck.

"If this is a bad time, I could come back later," Ash said.

"No." Carrie took her in, the clouds in her blue eyes lifting to reveal a hint of the sparkle Ash was used to seeing.

Ash felt warm under her gaze. Carrie's appraisal seemed more than casual, and Ash's memory suddenly flashed yet again to that moment in Mary's attic when they'd almost kissed. "Conversation with a jerk?" she asked, forcing herself present.

"It's a never-ending story in academia."

"Oh?" Ash asked, happy to listen to anything Carrie wanted to say.

"I'm sure you get the same attitude from some people. A

woman has to work twice as hard as a man to be taken seriously. For all the lip service they give to diversity, they still refuse to hire anyone who doesn't fit nicely with their old boys' club. They want professors who think like them and agree with their every idea. God forbid the status quo is challenged. It's academic inbreeding at its finest."

"After that phone conversation, I don't see how anyone could refuse to take you seriously." At a heavy sigh from Carrie, Ash insisted, "Really, I'm not sure if I understood what you were arguing about, but I would have given you anything you wanted."

"You're not a privileged, old, heterosexual male."

"I thank God for that every day." Ash felt her heart beat faster as a full-fledged smile spread across Carrie's face. That look of approval and amusement was enough to bring her to her knees. She was used to being the one who held the power in her interactions with women, but Carrie had turned the tables on her.

"I suppose you never have to think about workplace politics," Carrie said.

"Yeah, I'm my own boss, and I have a pretty big client base now. Mostly women and gay men. I usually don't have to work with anyone I don't want to."

"That would be a dream come true. I envy you not having to answer to anyone but yourself."

Carrie's appreciation seemed genuine, and her tone had taken on a hint of intimacy that wasn't there before. She came around to the front of her desk and leaned against it with her arms folded loosely across her chest. She wore a pair of brown slacks with a black V-neck sweater. The outfit made her look both professional and approachable, the picture of poise. Her shoes had just enough of a heel on them to make her the same height as Ash, leaving her beautiful blue eyes level with Ash's. Her proximity was enough to put Ash into sensory overload. Carrie was stunning, and it took every ounce of Ash's energy not to reach out and touch her.

"I don't really see why you can't have that," Ash said. "You're smart, attractive, and self-assured. What's stopping you from doing whatever you want?"

"It's not that easy here. I don't have tenure yet, and the big boys don't want to give it to me. If I'm not picture perfect for the next year, I could lose my job."

"What do you mean, picture perfect? Being a good teacher?" Ash thought she would have stayed in school much longer if she'd had more teachers who could command her attention like Carrie did.

Carrie let out a bitter sound that was probably meant to be a laugh. "Actually, that's really what they care about least sometimes. I have to be beyond reproach. Academically flawless, with at least four major publications."

Ash grimaced. They were back on topics she knew nothing about, and she couldn't help but wonder if Carrie would think less of her for that.

"And that's easy compared to categories such as service to the community, which can get pretty subjective. I sit on several university committees, though, so they'd have a hard time undermining that work. Still, none of it will make the slightest difference if I fall prey to the university's moral turpitude clauses. It's written so broadly that every aspect of my life can be scrutinized by the tenure committee."

Ash was beginning to put some of the pieces of the puzzle together. "So in other words, if you get a bad reputation for being unprofessional even in your personal life, they can bring that into work?"

"Absolutely. I'm in charge of shaping America's young minds." The sarcasm in her voice was biting.

Ash nodded solemnly as her heart began to sink. Carrie was a prisoner to her ambitions, and Ash's reputation could put her in jeopardy of losing everything. "So that's the famous liberalism I've heard of on college campuses."

"Well, at schools where women's studies is still scattered

across the curriculum rather than being centralized in its own department, we don't answer to other women's studies faculty. We answer to the different departments and ultimately to the dean of Art and Sciences."

"The guy you were yelling at?"

"That would be he." The corners of Carrie's mouth turned slightly upward in a display of defiance that Ash found extremely sexy. "Oh, listen to me. You stop by about bookshelves and get an earful of department politics."

"I don't mind." Ash put her hand gently on Carrie's shoulder. "I want to know what drives you, Carrie."

"Ash, I don't know how to say this really."

She stalled for a moment and Ash sensed that hint of hesitancy again. When Carrie looked into her eyes, Ash could see she didn't want to break the connection between them, but something was compelling her to do so nonetheless. Ash's heart beat in her throat as she waited for what was coming.

"Carrie doesn't drive me, Dr. Fletcher does."

Ash took a step back as the implications of what she'd just heard began to set in. "And Dr. Fletcher wants tenure, is that it?"

"Yes." Carrie nodded slowly. "She does."

"Well, then." Ash forced an enthusiasm she didn't feel. "I guess you're going to need room for a lot more books in here."

Carrie smiled at her, one of those smiles that made everything else disappear. "Thank you, Ash."

Ash's night was a restless one. She spent most of the evening selecting her lumber and preparing to build Carrie's bookcase. She chose a deep red oak for its durability, so that the structure would stand the test of time, as well as for its color, which she thought would bring a soothing presence to the institutionally white office. Each board for the frame was thickly cut so it would be heavy enough to anchor itself down. Then, to create a more uniform appearance, she took great care to make sure the oak's cathedral grains in each slat were cut at a similar angle. She measured each plank several times, wanting to be exact, and then handled her circular saw with delicate precision, taking care that not a single splinter was jarred out of place. She wanted the finished product to be perfect, so each piece had to be flawless.

It was well after midnight by the time she finally climbed into bed, but despite her physical exhaustion, thoughts of Carrie kept her awake. She tossed and turned for hours trying to find a way to reconcile her feelings with those Carrie had expressed earlier. She cursed herself for losing sleep over a woman. She was better than this. So Carrie had a job, who cared? Ash shook her head at the thought. This was exactly what Mary had been talking about. Ash was actually thinking of risking Carrie's career for the sake of her libido. How selfish could she get?

Yet although teaching obviously meant the world to Carrie, Ash could have sworn the desire she felt was not one-sided. Carrie wanted her, too. The sexual tension between them was too strong to be a figment of her imagination.

Doubt began to creep into that theory sometime before dawn, but Ash still had confidence. She might not know jack about Judith Butler, but she knew more than her fair share about desire, and she was certain the attraction was mutual. All she had to do was find a way to make Carrie realize that it was okay to act on her desires. They could be discreet until they got each other out of their systems. As Ash fell asleep, she still hadn't formulated a plan, but at least she felt like she was ready to try again.

"Well, you certainly look the part of the carpenter," Carrie said when Ash arrived at her office Wednesday morning.

"Thanks. I think."

Ash set down the stack of pre-cut shelves she'd hauled in with her. She was wearing well-worn denim painter pants over plaster-splattered work boots, and a tight white shirt covered by an unbuttoned and tattered long-sleeved flannel. She couldn't help but feel underdressed compared to the sleek black pantsuit Carrie was wearing. It was tailored perfectly to show off her curves, and the deep blue button-up dress shirt she wore under the jacket set off the dazzling color of her eyes. Her soft brown curls were pulled back loosely in a clip, which allowed small silver hoops to dangle unobstructed from her earlobes. Ash was captivated once again by the beauty of the woman sitting across the desk from her, and while she struggled to think of some appropriate way to convey that to Carrie, her charm failed.

Carrie glanced at the clock and rose from her desk, swinging a black satchel over her shoulder. "Well, I have classes all morning, so you can have the place to yourself."

Ash's heart sank. She'd been looking forward to some time alone with Carrie, especially within the small confines of the office. "Okay, well, have a good time shaping America's young minds," she said, trying not to let her disappointment show.

Carrie rolled her eyes, but Ash saw her mouth twitch slightly upward. Standing in front of the door, Ash felt like she should say something else, something smart, or funny, or cute. Anything, really. But in her indecision, she realized she was directly in Carrie's way. She stepped slightly aside just as Carrie moved in the same direction. It only took a split second to realize what she'd done and she moved back the other way, but Carrie had done the same. They both laughed at their own awkwardness before Ash took a step back, completely out of the office, giving Carrie room to pass.

"Thanks." Carrie didn't let her eyes meet Ash's as she brushed past her out into the hallway.

Ash wanted to start over and be her usual charming self. Instead, she felt inept once again. It was obvious that Carrie wasn't her usual conquest. She had the power to unnerve Ash in a way that was more than physical. The sexual tension coursing through her body was accentuated by an emotional vulnerability Ash didn't want to admit to. There had never been a woman who could make her try so hard to please, no one who could make her feel insecure about her ability to charm her way out of any situation. She was shocked by the power Carrie seemed to hold over her, but too intrigued to resist it.

For the next hour or more, she worked herself silly. The office was a smaller space than she was used to, and she spent twice as long on each section, measuring two and three times before fitting any piece into place. She reasoned that she was just being professional and that she wasn't dragging her feet in order to be around Carrie longer. At least when it came to carpentry, she knew what she was doing.

"Wow."

Ash looked up sharply to find Carrie propped in the doorway. Her gaze followed the solid oaken frame that now stretched tightly from the floor to the ceiling with both its base and top sanded and shelved in.

"I can't believe how much you've gotten done."

Ash avoided explaining that she should be finishing up by now. Carrie obviously didn't know how long it should take a professional to do a job like this. "I should be able to finish the bulk of the woodwork today. I'm busy tomorrow, but I can put the final touches on the woodwork on Friday. Hopefully, you'll have your bookcase by the end of the week."

"That sounds great." Carrie set her bag down and flopped in one of the chairs near the door. "But I'm leaving town on Friday, so I won't be here to let you in."

"Oh." Ash struggled not to show her disappointment. "Next week, then."

"Are you sure I'm not taking up too much of your time?"

"Not at all." Ash brushed sawdust off her pants and looked

up just in time to catch Carrie watching her. She could have sworn she saw a hint of lust in her eyes, but Carrie quickly averted her gaze.

Crossing to the window, she said, "It's hot in here."

After giving the window a couple of sharp tugs, she exhaled heavily when it didn't budge. Ash could tell she was flustered. Her knuckles turned white when she tried again, yet she didn't ask for help.

Ash strolled over and placed her arms on either side of Carrie. She took a deep breath of Carrie's shampoo before whispering, "It might help if you did this first."

She reached up and deftly flipped the lock, and the glass slid up quickly under Carrie's pressure, causing both of them to lose their balance slightly.

Carrie turned around, blushing. "Guess which one of us has a Ph.D."

"Oh, there is no doubt in my mind which one of us is the professor and which one of us is around to open windows." Ash leaned in closer so her body brushed against Carrie's.

"Ash…" Carrie started to pull away. She refused to make eye contact.

"Hold on." Ash took Carrie's hands in her own, feeling a spark start in her fingertips and spread rapidly through her limbs. "I have a confession to make."

"What?" Carrie tilted her chin, finally allowing their eyes to meet.

"I have absolutely no idea who Judith Butler is."

Carrie relaxed slightly, letting more of her body come into contact with Ash's.

"What?" Ash chuckled. "That wasn't what you were expecting?"

Carrie blushed and shook her head. "Actually, no. Judith Butler was the furthest thing from my mind."

"You were expecting me to do something more like this?"

Ash slid one arm around Carrie's waist and used her other hand to cup her face, gently pulling her in.

Carrie was not the only one caught off balance as their lips met. Ash felt dizzy and held Carrie tightly to keep herself from stumbling. The kiss that had started with the softest caress picked up speed as Ash felt Carrie's initial shock give way to hunger. Their lips parted and their tongues intertwined with a passion that went beyond anything Ash was used to from her many heated encounters. She was reaching up to run her hand though Carrie's soft curls the way she'd wanted to since the moment she saw her when there was a knock on the office door.

Ash spun around, and Carrie jumped out from behind her.

"Dr. Fletcher?" a woman called as the doorknob turned. "Are you coming to the meeting?"

Her voice seemed familiar. "Ash?" The woman stood just inside the door, blinking. "What are you doing here?"

When Ash failed to answer, Carrie said tensely, "Ash is building me some bookshelves, Rita."

"Oh." Rita's deep brown eyes swung back and forth between Ash and Carrie. "I didn't know you were a carpenter."

"I didn't know you were a professor." Ash wanted desperately to sound nonchalant. Carrie had probably figured out what had transpired between her and Rita already.

"I'm not," Rita answered slowly. "I'm a student. Dr. Fletcher is my advisor."

The only thing Carrie heard was the sound of her own pulse still beating erratically from the feel of Ash's kiss.

"We need to start working on the logistics for our annual Take Back The Night rally," Rita said, bringing the meeting to order. "We have to reserve the space on the quad and rent a sound system."

Carrie served as the faculty advisor for the executive board of the Feminist Majority Leadership Alliance. They met weekly to discuss meetings topics for their general membership and to plan campus-wide events. It was a part of her job Carrie usually looked forward to because it meant spending time with bright, motivated young women, and it gave her a chance to develop a mentor relationship with each of them. The FMLA students turned to her for advice and guidance in situations both at school and in their personal lives, and they often stayed in contact with her well after they graduated.

Under normal circumstances she followed the discussion closely, but today she couldn't focus on anything other than the kiss she'd just shared with Ash. Part of her wanted to be furious that Ash had kissed her. She thought she'd made it perfectly plain that she wanted to keep their interaction platonic. At the same time, she realized it was unfair to pin all the blame on Ash. The woman had a raw sexuality that was purely magnetic, and despite ample warning from others, Carrie found her hard to resist. Ash could be so disarming and so sexy all at once, it would be dishonest to pretend she wasn't interested. She also genuinely enjoyed the time they spent together.

"Carrie?" Rita's voice interrupted her thoughts.

The students were looking at her expectantly.

"I'm sorry, what?"

"We just wanted to know who we should call to have a little stage set up for the rally," one of the girls repeated.

"Oh, that would be the facilities office," Carrie answered, embarrassed to have been caught daydreaming.

She hoped the students couldn't tell what she was thinking about, though she felt like it was written all over her face. Surely her lips were swollen from the kiss. *Was that really just a kiss?* If so, then she had never been kissed before. She'd certainly never felt like this in the past. Her breathing quickened as she remembered the feel of their bodies connecting. Ash had been so tender and passionate, all her logic and reasoning had left her completely. The minute their lips met, a current of desire overwhelmed her senses. She hadn't tried to resist; she didn't want the feeling to end. Even now, her body ached from the withdrawal.

"That's in the student center, right, Carrie?"

"No, the facilities office is under the buildings and maintenance department."

Several of the girls exchanged uncomfortable glances. "We were talking about getting flyers printed up for the event."

"Oh." Carrie flushed. "Yes, the printer is in the student center. Just have it billed to the organization's account."

The students resumed their discussion, but Carrie didn't miss the suspicious look Rita gave her. *Oh, no. She's figured it out.*

Carrie was horrified by that possibility. She'd been so caught up in the heat of the moment that she'd failed to fully process the awkward exchange between Rita and Ash. There was obviously a history between them; it was plain to see from the looks on their faces. Was the same look on hers? Would Rita recognize it? What about the others? Would they know? How many of them had been placed in similar situations by Ash?

Carrie wasn't naïve. She knew her lesbian students spent a great deal of their weekends at the Triangle Club and that they weren't looking for long-term, monogamous relationships. The thought that their dating pool had suddenly combined with hers made her stomach churn. How many of her students had Ash slept with? Would Rita tell them that their trusted advisor had given in to the same temptation? It didn't matter that she hadn't actually slept with Ash. Rumors about a usually poised and professional professor in a compromising position were too juicy for anyone to check the facts. By the time the news made its way to the dean...

Carrie felt dizzy. A rumor like that was exactly what he was looking for. It would undermine her academic credibility by blurring the boundaries between her and her students, and show a moral weakness for meaningless sexual encounters. It didn't matter that they had just kissed, and it didn't matter that the kiss was far from meaningless to her. The mere appearance of impropriety was all Dean Phillips needed.

Carrie stood abruptly, fighting off a wave of nausea. "Girls, I'm not feeling well today. I think I'm going to head home for the afternoon."

"Okay," one of them said, "I'll just e-mail you my meeting notes."

"Feel better," another chimed in.

Carrie mumbled her thanks as she headed out the door. For a few seconds she hesitated, staring toward her office, but she had her satchel with her and didn't have to return for keys. The last thing she needed right now was to see Ash, and if she slipped out now she would have almost an entire week before having to face her again. Hopefully with some time and space, she would be able to get a grip on herself.

"Ash? You haven't heard a word I've said, have you?"

"What? Yeah, of course I have." Ash tried to focus her attention on Mary.

"You big fibber. Something happen today that you want to talk about?"

Something had happened, all right, but did she want to talk about it? Ash wasn't sure. She didn't know whether to be mad at Rita for bursting in on them, or herself for sleeping with one of Carrie's students. She was also irrationally angry at Carrie for making her worry about something that had happened before they met. She'd waited for hours for Carrie to come back to the office, and even considered going to look for her, but there was no way she was going to chase after a woman she barely knew.

It didn't matter how amazing the kiss had been. So she'd left the office, and now, several hours later, she was having dinner with Mary and Sharon.

"Weren't you supposed to meet with Carrie about her shelves this afternoon?" Mary asked.

Sharon looked up from her pork chop and green beans. "Yeah. How did that go?"

"It was fine." Ash stuffed a fork full of beans into her mouth to avoid having to answer any more questions.

"Are you and her…?" Sharon raised her eyebrows.

"No," Mary cut in. "They aren't." Turning to Ash, she asked, "Are you?"

"No!"

"No? Or not yet?" Sharon grinned.

"For crying out loud, can we talk about something else?" Ash muttered.

Sharon shrugged. "I didn't realize you were so sensitive about her."

"I'm not. I just don't want to discuss my relationship status every time we eat together. Okay?"

An uneasy silence stretched between them. Ash could almost hear her friends thinking out loud. Mary had to know that something was up. She could read her like a book, and Sharon knew her well enough to know she didn't get bent out of shape about women. She was sure they could both see the effect Carrie was having on her. Ash struggled to come up with an innocuous conversation starter, but when she failed to think of a less loaded topic she pretended to be engrossed in her dinner until they were mercifully interrupted by the ringing of the phone.

Sharon got up and answered it, her voice only partially distinguishable through the kitchen wall. Obviously she wasn't thrilled with whoever was on the other end of the line. Ash glanced at Mary, who just shrugged.

After a minute or two, Sharon came back and Ash could

tell by the look on her face that she wasn't happy. "That was the store."

"Oh, don't tell me—"

"I can't help it. I have to work this Saturday. Dave threw out his back."

Mary dropped her napkin on her plate and immediately started cleaning. "You promised you'd be off this weekend. The kids from the center have been looking forward to this camping trip all summer."

"I don't want to work, but I have to."

Mary gathered up a handful of dishes and carried them into the kitchen. The stiffness of her shoulders made her anger plain.

"What's the deal?" Ash asked Sharon.

"I promised to help chaperone the youth center camping trip. So Dave throws out his back and I'm the only other manager in town. Great."

"Why can't they just get one of the other volunteers to go?"

"It's Amy and Tara's anniversary, so they're in Chicago," Mary interjected from the other room.

"And Michael?"

Mary's voice filled with frustration. "Michael will be there, but that makes only three of us. We need at least four adults."

"Who's the third?"

"I'd tell you, but you don't want to talk about her," Mary snapped.

"Come on, Mary," Sharon said. "You're mad at me. Don't take it out on her."

Mary returned to face her partner, hands on hips. "You promised you'd take this weekend off. The kids were counting on you. I was counting on you. Now we're going to have to cancel after three months of planning."

"I know that, and I feel awful, but what do you want me to do? I could wheel Dave's bed into the store, but I'm pretty sure that isn't going to solve anything."

"I don't care what you or Dave do. I just want you do to something."

Ash thought for just a split second about the prospect of spending the weekend in a tent with Carrie, and said, "I'll do it."

"What?" Sharon and Mary stared at her as if she'd lost her mind.

"I'll chaperone the camping trip with you."

Mary regarded her suspiciously. "Why?"

"You're my best friend, and it's important to you," Ash said with conviction. "And I survived a Saturday night at the center. What's one more weekend?"

"Is this about Carrie?"

Ash felt her checks flush. She didn't want to consider the full consequences of her offer. "I thought you needed a chaperone. Do you want my help or not?"

"Mary," Sharon cut in cautiously, "you said yourself how much you wanted Ash to get involved in the center."

Mary rolled her eyes. "Don't use her to get yourself out of trouble."

Sharon wisely shut her mouth, and she and Ash waited while Mary seemed to be considering her options. She finally gave a heavy sigh. "All right. I'm still not convinced your motives are pure, but the kids are really looking forward to this trip. Can you be ready to leave at two on Friday afternoon?"

"Sure." Ash nodded even though it was only true in the literal sense. She could certainly be packed, but when it came to the feelings that accompanied any time spent with Carrie, she doubted she would ever be truly ready.

Chapter Eight

I'm going to put those ponchos in my wagon. Why don't you look over this?" Mary handed a map of Alliance Rock State Park to Carrie.

"It's not supposed to rain this weekend," Carrie responded absentmindedly.

Mary tucked the bright yellow rain gear into the tightly packed storage area of her Subaru station wagon regardless. "Which area should we head for?" she asked.

Carrie unfolded the map and scanned the page, completely failing to take anything in. "Um, the one closest to a real bathroom?"

"All the camping areas have bathrooms. Are you even looking at the map?" Mary pointed to the restroom signs next to each tent area.

"I'm not some kind of nature lesbian," Carrie protested. "I'm one of the purely academic types. Why don't you let Sharon decide where we are going to stay?"

"About that." Mary lifted guilty eyes.

Carrie regarded her suspiciously. "What?"

"Sharon can't make it, so Ash is coming along."

"Ash?"

"We need another adult on the trip and she was the only one available on such short notice."

"When did you plan on mentioning this to me?"

"I didn't think it would be a big deal." Mary avoided looking her in the eye.

She obviously knew something had happened between them, Carrie thought, cursing herself for the thousandth time. First Rita, now Mary. Before long the entire town would know how weak she was. It was a high price to pay for a simple kiss.

Maybe simple wasn't exactly the right term. It had been two days and Carrie still couldn't forget the feel of Ash's lips on hers, or the easy way their bodies fit together. She had lain awake at night trying to analyze how things had gotten so out of control so quickly, but she hadn't come up with any reasonable answer. In fact, her attraction to Ash seemed to defy logic in every single way. She couldn't trust her body when Ash was around, and apparently she couldn't depend on her mental control, either. The thought of spending an entire weekend around her was completely unnerving. She was going to have to try to maintain a safe distance and cling to any professional reserve she had left.

"It's not a big deal," she lied to both Mary and herself. *Everything will be fine as long as I don't look at her.*

"Good," Mary said resolutely, "because here she comes."

Ash pulled the Mustang into Mary's driveway and hopped out to greet her. She glanced over at Carrie hopefully but was disheartened when she turned away. She hadn't exactly expected a warm welcome, but she'd hoped Carrie would at least acknowledge her.

"Are you sure you still want to do this?" Mary asked.

No, Ash thought. Now that she'd had more time to think, she'd started to wonder what she had gotten herself into. She didn't like teenagers, she didn't like camping, and she certainly didn't expect to like combining the two. She'd also realized she would probably have to spend as much time with Tess as she did with Carrie. Then there was the Rita factor. Ash had to assume from Carrie's disappearance on Wednesday that she knew about Rita and wasn't pleased. Maybe Carrie wouldn't even speak to her. Ash shook off that thought. She didn't care what it took. There was no way she was spending a weekend in a tent with Tess and not getting through to Carrie.

"I said I'd go, and I meant it," she answered, then added, "I'll be fine."

"I hope so, because here comes Michael with some of the kids."

Ash turned around to see a Chevy Tahoe. Michael looked even smaller behind the wheel of such a large vehicle. "Is that his car?" she asked.

Mary nodded. "Not a word about overcompensation, please."

"You said it, not me." Ash chuckled as the new arrivals piled out into Mary's front yard.

Michael approached, casting a quick puzzled look in Ash's direction. "I'm surprised to see you back for more."

"Good to see you too, Mike. Nice car." Ash was not quite able to hide the sarcasm in her voice.

He eyed her suspiciously. "Thanks."

"What have you got in there?" she asked, fighting a grin. "Obviously a V-8. Is it the Vortec forty-eight-hundred or did you go for the fifty-three-hundred?"

"I went with the leather interior," Michael said so confidently that it took everything Ash had not to laugh.

"Good for you, Mikey."

"Michael has impeccable taste," Mary cut in, shooting Ash a look that said that was enough teasing for now.

"So are you our other driver?" Michael asked.

"Oh, I don't think so," Ash answered.

Mary cocked her head to the side as if she was thinking about it. "Well, I guess your car is bigger than Carrie's. She's just got a hatchback."

Ash felt herself shudder both at the mention of Carrie's name and the word *hatchback*. She hated the idea of driving her pride and joy into the woods, but the thought of being in the Mustang with Carrie by her side was enough to win her over. Mary and Michael spent a few minutes figuring out who would take which boys and girls. After they'd settled on the passenger lists, Mary strolled over to Carrie. Ash watched their conversation from a distance, trying to gauge what they were saying by their body language.

"You're not her type," came a smug voice, and Tess set down a cooler full of snacks and drinks.

"Want me to put that in the trunk?" Ash offered, ignoring the comment.

"You're so chivalrous." Tess feigned a swoon.

Ash had to smile. The kid had a sense of humor; she could give her that.

A girl Ash hadn't met yet approached them. She greeted Tess before saying, "Hi, Ash. I'm Michelle Marx. Mary said I should ride with you."

Ash returned the girl's smile. She looked about Tess's age, but a few inches shorter. Her brunette hair was shoulder length and she wore jeans and a light blue sweatshirt. She kept her eyes on Tess the whole time she spoke to Ash, a fact that didn't escape any of them. Ash told her to put her stuff in the car.

"You can take Tess with you," she added teasingly.

"Fine." Tess shrugged. "But if I'm going to ride in the Mustang, I've got shotgun."

Ash shook her head. "Not on your life."

"Are you saving that spot for me?"

Ash's heart jerked into a rapid pace as Carrie walked toward her. The comment wasn't exactly the warm welcome she had hoped for, but it was a start. "If you want it, it's all yours."

Carrie shrugged. "Mary made the car assignments, not me."

"Mary gets what Mary wants," Ash replied, suppressing a grin.

Carrie brushed past Ash without a blink. "Sounds like someone else I met recently."

❖

The drive to Alliance Rock State Park took just over an hour. That is to say that it took just over an hour to get there when driving the speed limit, which Mary insisted they do even though Carrie could tell it was killing Ash to go so slow in the Mustang.

"This is a great car," Michelle said as soon as they got on the road.

"Thanks," Ash replied. "Are you into cars?"

"Not really. I mean, I like to look at them, but I don't really know anything about them."

Ash smiled one of those wonderfully disarming smiles that made it so hard for Carrie to remember why she was mad at her in the first place. "Cars are easy to figure out. Everything is connected to something else in a logical chain. If you just follow the logical steps, the car will always come through for you. That's what I like about them."

"It also doesn't hurt if the car is a total chick magnet," Tess added.

Ash's reaction was surprisingly nonchalant. "Tess, if you need a car to help you meet women, then you are going after the wrong kind of women."

"Sure, I'll bet you've never turned down any backseat action."

"Tess," Carrie cut in. It wasn't that she disagreed with anything Tess was saying, she just didn't want to be reminded of Ash's reputation.

"What? She's not denying it," Tess said.

"What Ash does in her personal time is no one's business but her own," Carrie stated flatly.

"Hers and the people she does it with," Tess said under her breath.

Carrie got the sneaking suspicion that the conversation wasn't really about the car at all. Was Tess talking about her? Had she figured out that something happened with Ash? Could everyone feel the tension between them? She was working hard to appear neutral in front of the kids, but it wasn't easy to do with Ash sitting so close.

The rest of the drive was spent discussing mundane things, and Carrie was glad when the trip was over and everyone went about their separate tasks. She needed some time to think and she couldn't focus clearly while watching Ash out of the corner of her eye. She didn't mean to keep looking at her, but the woman was just too magnetic to ignore. Her deeply tanned skin and dark hair along with her practically flawless build and knee-weakening smile made her the very embodiment of tall, dark, and handsome. How could anyone be rational when looking at her?

When they all got out of the car Carrie purposefully put some distance between herself and Ash. *This is getting ridiculous,* she thought. I'm thirty-three years old, not some schoolgirl fawning over the local heartthrob. *I've got to find a way to get my composure back.* There was no way she could spend a whole weekend like this. She'd worked with demeaning deans and unruly students for years and managed to keep a professional relationship with all of them; surely a civil tone during a three-day camping trip wasn't too much to ask. If only Ash would cooperate with her.

❖

Mary got them checked in. The boys unloaded the cars, and Ash helped Michael set up the tents while Carrie talked to the girls about the sleeping arrangements.

Ash listened to their discussion as best she could while still trying to keep Michael from destroying the tents. "There's going to be one chaperone to each tent," Carrie said, reciting who was sleeping where. Ash would be sharing with Erin and Kevin, who weren't thrilled with the coed tent, but Carrie shook her head.

"Nobody will be doing anything but sleeping in those tents," she said firmly, and Ash couldn't help but smile.

She liked the thought of Carrie sleeping in the tent next door, but Carrie didn't seem to return the sentiment. She quickly went about her business, barely acknowledging Ash's presence. Ash frowned at the cold shoulder but she was determined not to act desperate. She would bide her time until the right opportunity presented itself. She wanted to be in control of the situation, and she was almost able to convince herself that she was.

After everyone had settled in and there was a nice fire going, Ash finally took a moment to look around. The sun had faded below the horizon, and the pink streaks left behind cast a low light across their campsite. Their tents were set up on the edge of a line of timber that got thicker with each step into it. The leaves were almost at their peak color, with reds, oranges, and yellows overshadowing the few remaining patches of green. Several trails were cut into the woods, and although she hadn't explored any of them, she knew most led to the large lake at the center of the park.

The teens had gone to explore the area, with Michael tagging along to keep an eye on them. Mary was cleaning up some of the snacks that had been scattered around the campsite, and Annie was entertaining Carrie by picking up every stick or leaf she came across and then attempting to put it in her mouth. Ash felt herself melt at the sound of Carrie's laughter. Annie was obviously displeased with the taste of a twig she chewed before anyone could stop her, and her expressions were priceless.

As Mary scooped up her daughter, Ash strolled over to Carrie. She felt her stiffen, and Carrie didn't even look at her. Ash cringed at how she lost all ability to be articulate in Carrie's presence.

After what seemed like an eternity of tense silence, Carrie said, "Ash, what happened on Wednesday—"

"I'm sorry about Rita," Ash blurted out.

Carrie winced. "This isn't about Rita."

Ash cocked an eyebrow but waited before saying anything else.

"At least not directly," Carrie continued, as if carefully weighing her words.

"I can explain." Ash could hear the desperation creeping into her voice. Unsettled, she said, "There's nothing going on between us."

"You don't have anything to explain. I honestly don't want to know about it either way." Carrie tried to force a smile, but Ash sensed a hint of uncertainty behind the words.

"If you say so," Ash responded tentatively.

"I can't afford any distractions in my life right now," Carrie continued. "I'm up for tenure next year, and while that might not mean anything to you, it's something that I've been working toward for a long time."

"I understand how important your job is to you."

"No, you don't," Carrie said firmly but without venom, "or you wouldn't have put me in a position to have to say this, but that's over now. We both need to move on before we do something we can't undo."

Ash felt sick to her stomach. "Carrie, I don't want to get in the way of your dreams, but—"

"Good, then don't." Carrie cut her short. "I want everyone to have a good time here, and for that to happen we have to clear this tension between us. Can we just forget the whole thing ever happened and go about our weekend?"

"You can do that?" A dull ache settled in Ash's chest.

"I think it would be for the best."

Ash nodded, hoping that Carrie couldn't sense how upset she was. "All right, then."

After Carrie walked away, it took everything Ash had not to sulk for the rest of the evening. She refused to accept that she was hurt. Carrie didn't seem to feel the way she did about the kiss they'd shared, the kiss that had sent Ash's whole world spinning. How could they just ignore it and pretend it had never happened? Ash had plenty of experience walking away from good sex, she reasoned, even great sex. She just had to keep telling herself that this was no different.

She shifted to a log near the fire, took a marshmallow from the plastic bag Mary passed around, and roasted it in silence, watching the flames dance. When she felt someone sit down beside her, she dared to hope for a moment but groaned inwardly when she looked up. Tess stared at her expectantly. Her loose blond hair swept across her shoulders and she'd changed into jeans and a tight-fitting long-sleeved T-shirt obviously chosen to show off the shape of her body. Ash couldn't help but feel the attention to her appearance was not coincidental.

"What's up, Tess?" she asked as casually as she could.

"Isn't this a little boring for your tastes?" Tess cocked her head to one side.

Ash shrugged. "I suppose it's kind of tame."

"I have an idea to help spice it up."

"I'm sure you do."

"Wanna hear it?" Tess slid a little closer.

"No."

"Maybe you just need a little convincing." Tess raised her eyebrows suggestively.

Ash shook her head. "Tess, you're wasting your time practicing on me. Why don't you aim those teenage hormones at someone who'll be interested?"

Tess sighed and gave in to a full-fledged pout.

Ash fought to suppress a smile. "Oh, that's mature."

"Bite me."

"Seriously, you're an attractive, out-and-proud baby dyke. Any of these girls would love for you to ask them out."

"I don't want any of *these* girls," Tess said.

"Why not? Michelle's cute and she's obviously got it bad for you."

Tess rolled her eyes.

"She wanted to ride with you in the car, and she's going to be sharing the tent with you and Carrie. She's gone out of her way all day to be wherever you are," Ash continued.

"She follows me around, I get it."

"So? What are you waiting for? Ask her out."

"I don't want to date, I want to fuck," Tess said flatly.

Ash was speechless, taken aback by the blunt words coming from the mouth of the sixteen-year-old. It wasn't that she didn't understand the sentiment. She'd lived by it herself for years. But something cold and detached about the way Tess spoke made her shiver. Before she could come up with a reply, the girl glared at her and stormed off.

"I see you two are getting along well," Carrie said, plopping down a few feet away.

Startled that Carrie was talking to her, Ash said, "She doesn't like being told no."

"Tess can be very assertive."

"Is that what you call it?"

"She's got a good heart." Carrie's voice was strained, as if she was making an effort to talk. "Sometimes it's just hard to see through all the walls she puts up."

"If you say so." Ash noticed that she'd burned her marshmallow. "Damn, I was so distracted this is charcoal now."

She scraped away the charred remains and put another one on the stick, aware the whole time of Carrie's eyes on her. She could feel the tension in her and wondered why she was suddenly making an effort to talk. Ash had half expected her to be distant all weekend. The change of heart was a relief, but also a mystery.

As if they normally talked in this cozy manner, Carrie said, "Her dad isn't around, and her mom is pretty hard on her. She's just acting out in the only way she knows how."

"You don't have to justify her to me. She can act out all she wants. I just don't want her directing it at me."

"She's directing it at you because she can't figure out if she wants to date you or be you," Carrie said.

Ash turned her marshmallow over the fire, thankful to have something to look at since Carrie still wasn't meeting her eyes. "She doesn't want to *date*. She made that perfectly clear. And as for 'being' me, that's some pretty heavy psychological crap."

"Is that for me?" Carrie indicated the golden marshmallow. Her tone was suddenly lighter.

Ash glanced at her in surprise. "If you want it."

Without thinking, she plucked the marshmallow from the stick and reached across to pop it into Carrie's mouth. It was hard to tell if Carrie was blushing or if her cheeks were just red from the fire. Ash licked the melted sugar from her fingers and watched Carrie's tongue slide across her lips.

Aware of a strange heat rushing beneath her skin, Ash asked, "How was it?"

Carrie stared at her. "Perfect."

Ash pulled another marshmallow from the bag. "Do I get to have this one, or are you still hungry?"

"I think it's your turn," Carrie said. "And I'll even toast it since you seem to lose your concentration so easily."

Ash's heart pounded as Carrie took the stick from her and speared the marshmallow. Impulsively, she asked, "Why are you doing this?"

"Doing what?"

Ash didn't know how to answer. She decided her imagination was working overtime. Carrie wasn't flirting with her, she was just trying to pretend everything was normal between them for the sake of the others. She'd made it clear that she didn't want what had happened between them to spoil the trip.

Resigning herself to keeping up the charade of a platonic friendship, Ash said, "Nothing. I'm just happy you decided to keep me company."

"There's no reason why I shouldn't. I plan to enjoy the weekend."

"Me, too." Ash almost fell off her log when Carrie shifted to sit next to her.

"Ready?" Carrie held the stick so that Ash could bite the marshmallow.

Ash chewed awkwardly under Carrie's steady gaze. Her stomach churned at the thought that Carrie would only have to move a few inches and their thighs would be in contact. She sat very still, her breathing not quite even. Carrie reached for the bag of marshmallows as if it was the most natural thing in the world to let her arm graze past Ash's body. When she settled back onto the log, the small gap between them closed and Ash could feel the lift of Carrie's shoulders as she breathed and the warmth of their flesh where it connected. She stole a quick sideways look at Carrie and saw no sign of unease on her face.

For a few minutes, they were quiet, watching the fire. As she relaxed, Ash realized how much she liked the feel of Carrie sitting next to her. It was comfortable, easy. She even let herself wonder what it would be like to have this feeling on a regular basis. The thought disturbed her. She had closed the door on that possibility a long time ago. She knew who she was and didn't pretend to be anyone else. Anyone who knew her knew she wasn't the type to settle down.

It wasn't that she couldn't understand Carrie's perspective. Of course she didn't want to risk her livelihood over a woman who had nothing to offer except some short-term fun in bed; she had too much to lose and little to gain. For some reason, Ash found that truth hard to accept. Puzzled, she stared at Carrie's hands as she held the stick over the fire once more. She couldn't believe what she was thinking. That she wanted to take Carrie's hand and hold it. She wanted to feel close to her, to somehow make this moment more intimate even if that didn't involve sex.

A shock of dismay rippled past the back of her throat, making her choke slightly. She'd never had a feeling like this in her life. What in hell was going on with her? Stunned, she got to her feet and mumbled something about being tired. She made her way quickly to her tent and crawled into her sleeping bag, shutting her eyes tightly to close out the image of Carrie in the firelight.

You have got to get a grip, she told herself. She couldn't keep playing these games with Carrie, there was too much at stake. Being close to her also made Ash feel vulnerable, and she couldn't handle that. It was time for her to get back in control. She'd never questioned the choices she'd made in her life. She liked her freedom and wasn't about to give that up for anyone. As for Carrie, she could make all the declarations she wanted, but as of tomorrow, Ash was putting the relationship back on her own terms.

CHAPTER NINE

Carrie was up earlier than most of the teenagers, so she made the most of her quiet time. Grabbing a fresh change of clothes and her blow-dryer, she headed for the closest thing to civilization, the camp's community bathroom. The shower wasn't bad at all, and as she soaked in the warm water, she was thankful to remove the smell of last night's campfire. It wasn't just the scent of smoke that bothered her, it was the memories. But those proved harder to wash away. Carrie wasn't completely sure what she'd been thinking when she approached Ash.

She had initially headed that way to check on Tess and had rationalized the start of her conversation with Ash as concern for the teenager as well. She really did still hope that Ash and Tess would connect on some meaningful level, but that wasn't the only reason she sought out Ash's company. At some point very early in their conversation she'd forgotten about Tess completely. Ash tended to have that effect on her. She had been unable to stop herself from flirting a little bit.

Flirting? Carrie let out an embarrassed groan. She didn't flirt. She had a Ph.D., for God's sake. She was known for being poised, professional, the very image of respectability. Why did all of that disappear any time she was around Ashton Clarke? Her behavior at the fireside last night had been so unlike her. Not to mention how unfair it had been to Ash. So much for sending a clear message about keeping their relationship platonic. She was supposed to be a strong, self-possessed woman, and instead of acting like one she had behaved exactly like she expected one of her students to. Just like Rita.

At that thought Carrie abruptly turned off the shower. She refused to compare herself to Rita. The two of them weren't alike in any way. She wasn't going to let Ash turn her into just another fawning admirer. She was in control of her behavior, and she was certainly capable of maintaining a friendly relationship without letting her feelings become sexual.

Ash almost turned and walked the other way when she exited the shower stall and found Carrie bent over the sink trying to dry the underside of her unruly brown hair. She wore jeans that hugged her hips ever so slightly and a loose-fitting sweater that looked almost as soft as the hair she was fighting so hard to tame.

Carrie jumped slightly when she noticed Ash. She switched off the blow-dryer and ran her hand through her hair.

"Sorry, I didn't mean to scare you," Ash said.

"It's okay." Carrie examined her reflection in the mirror before giving in to a look of resignation. "There's only so much I can do with it some days. Of course, being in the wilderness doesn't help much."

"You could have fooled me." Ash took a step closer and made eye contact with Carrie via the mirror. She liked the reflection she saw, the two of them standing together over a bathroom sink. "I think you look great."

Carrie rolled her eyes and faced Ash as if she was about to say something, but then she seemed to think better of it. Ash caught a glimpse of herself in the mirror and realized her white T-shirt and boxers had gotten damp from the steam and were looking rather translucent under the florescent lights. Carrie's eyes flashed as they moved over her, and Ash couldn't help but feel pleased that she was noticing her body. She fought to suppress a smile. Carrie just looked so damn kissable when she let down her guard, and it took all the restraint Ash had not to pull her close right then and there.

"Sleep well?" Carrie asked, putting away her toiletries as if she knew she'd been caught staring.

"Yes, I slept fine, thanks."

In fact, Ash had slept horribly. There was nothing pleasant about sleeping in a small tent between two teenagers. The ground was hard and uneven, and it felt like she was lying directly on a baseball-sized rock. She couldn't move, however, due to the way she was crammed into a sleeping bag with Erin's elbow jabbing her on one side and Kevin snoring loudly on the other.

Then there was the fact that she was wearing pajamas. She hadn't worn pajamas since she'd gotten her own place, and the sweatpants and T-shirt seemed to bunch up with every move she made. The entire situation was unbearably constricting. For an expert in avoiding actually *sleeping* with someone else, being at close quarters with two other people made for an excruciatingly long night. Ash wanted to think discomfort was the only cause of her broken sleep, but the other reason was standing in front of her, cheeks slightly pink.

"Well, I guess I'd better get back to the camp," Carrie said.

Ash intended to play it cool, but the right words wouldn't come. "Why don't you wait and we'll walk back together."

As soon as she'd spoken, she felt foolish, as though this was high school and she'd just offered to carry a girl's books. The expression on Carrie's face was no help. Ash read uncertainty but also something else. Carrie bit her lower lip, as if she was trying to hold something in. Ash wondered if she would ever be able to read her the way she read other women. Most of the time she found Carrie utterly perplexing.

"Okay," Carrie said dryly. "But only if you're planning to

get dressed. I'm not sure how Tess would cope seeing you in your shorts."

Ash stared down at herself. "I'll just be a second."

She quickly unzipped the duffel bag and pulled on a pair of jeans over the boxer shorts. Carrie hadn't moved yet and Ash took that as a good sign. She pulled a worn gray sweatshirt over her head and slipped her feet back into her boots. With a quick glance in the mirror, she flattened down a strand of dark brown hair and was ready to go.

Carrie gave her an amused look as they headed for the door. "That was quick."

Ash shrugged. "I'm pretty low maintenance."

"Why do I find that hard to believe?" Carrie asked softly.

Ash had a feeling the question was meant for herself.

After a game of ultimate Frisbee that could only be described as a showcase for her fumbling and lack of concentration, Ash spent lunch trying to stay focused on the conversation going on around her. She sat intentionally at a different table from Carrie, with Michael and some of the kids. Carrie was with Mary and the other teens outside of the concession stand at the park. It took all of Ash's will not to look at her constantly.

She had messed up during the Frisbee game, and she knew it. She hadn't been thinking. After playing like an idiot for an hour or so, she'd finally managed to catch a wayward pass from Carrie, to end the game. It had been so natural to swing her into a bear hug, Ash had completely forgotten that everyone was watching. As if that wasn't bad enough, she'd wanted to kiss her like they were the only ones there, and almost did. Carrie had tensed up immediately and nothing actually happened, but still the event terrified Ash. She was good with women. Getting them into bed was effortless and she was always fully aware of what she was doing. Every move was practiced and controlled. But Carrie had shaken her usual composure, and that was exactly what Ash had sworn to avoid the night before. She had to stay in control of her feelings or someone would get hurt.

"What about you, Ash?" Michael asked.

"What?" Ash realized she'd zoned out again.

"Are you going to hike or boat?"

"Oh, I'm not sure. Is that what we're doing this afternoon?"

"Yeah, half of us are going to hike up to an overlook where you can see the whole state park, and the others are canoeing around the lake."

"I can do whatever you need," Ash said, not really caring.

"Well, Carrie and I are going on the hike, so you should probably boat."

"Why do you say that?" Ash asked quickly, afraid that Carrie didn't want to be around her after the embarrassing moment during the Frisbee game.

Michael raised an eyebrow. "Mary can't be the only adult on the lake."

"Oh." Ash felt embarrassed that she hadn't come to that conclusion herself. "Sure. That's fine."

She glanced across at Mary, who appeared to be getting ready to leave. Excusing herself, Ash stalked over to join her, convinced that everyone was staring. They went to the boat rental area and checked out two canoes and six life jackets. While Mary helped Annie into her little life jacket, Ash checked out the canoe she'd be paddling. The young park ranger helping them had followed her to the dock. Ash checked her name badge. Casey Hanson.

"So, do you do a lot of canoeing?" Casey asked.

"Not really. I haven't been since I was a kid." Ash put on the life jacket and started adjusting the straps.

"You've got a beautiful day for it," the ranger said, looking at Ash instead of the scenery.

"Yeah." Ash fastened the buckles and gave the straps one more tug.

"Just be careful you don't tip it. The water is only about forty-five or fifty degrees today."

"Well, I don't plan on trying to drown myself out there."

"Good. There are better ways to get wet." The ranger's voice was slightly lower than before.

Ash looked at her properly for the first time. Casey Hanson was about her height with sandy blond hair and light hazel eyes. Her body was deeply tanned underneath her forest green ranger uniform, and she had her sleeves rolled up, revealing tightly toned biceps.

"I'd go with you if I didn't have to work." Casey reached out and gave a gentle tug on Ash's jacket, transparently pretending to check that it was secure. Her fingers brushed gently against Ash's side, lingering just long enough to be noticed.

"Yeah, maybe some other time." Ash smiled, her confidence bolstered by the attention she was used to getting. This was exactly the type of interaction she thrived on.

"Well, I get off at six tonight. We could go then. I know some great little spots around here that you can only get to by boat. I'd love to show you."

"Trust me, you can't take her anywhere she hasn't already been." Tess pushed between them onto the boat dock.

Ash looked up, her jaw clenched at yet another interruption from the teenager. But Tess wasn't alone. Carrie and Michelle stood just behind her. Ash's heart sank at the look on Carrie's face. How long had she been standing there? From her expression it had been long enough to realize what was going on.

With a quick look in their direction, Casey said, "My offer's good as long as you want." Ash barely noticed her walk off. Her attention was focused solely on Carrie and the mix of hurt and embarrassment she saw in her beautiful blue eyes.

"Tess and I decided to stay and canoe with you," Michelle said. She sounded apologetic, obviously aware of the tension.

"Sure." Ash tried not to appear rattled. "Why don't you put on some life jackets and climb in."

As the girls got themselves organized, Ash and Carrie were left staring at each other again. Ash struggled to think of something she could say or do to defuse the situation but, as usual, Carrie's presence completely killed her self-confidence. The ability she always had to put women at ease vanished. The things she would normally say in a situation like this sounded phony and pathetic when she imagined saying them to Carrie. She hated feeling so exposed.

"Well, have a good ride," Carrie finally said.

"Yeah." Ash sighed. "Enjoy your hike."

"Thank you," Carrie said tightly, and once more, Ash was just standing there, watching her walk away.

Without thinking, she gave in to a reckless urge and called, "Carrie, wait." She jogged a few steps to close the distance between them. "I've, uh…I've had a good time with you this weekend."

Carrie stopped walking. She seemed surprised by the comment.

"I just didn't want you to get the wrong impression about what you saw back there." Ash explained awkwardly. "I wanted to make sure you knew that."

Carrie gave her a quizzical smile. "I'm glad."

Her features began to soften as Ash held her gaze. Her blue eyes reflected the sunlight in much the same way as the lake behind her, and her curls rustled slightly in the gentle breeze. Ash felt the familiar urge to touch her. At that moment she wanted more than anything to run her fingers through Carrie's hair, but instead she repeated, "Have fun on the hike."

"Thanks." Carrie walked away, leaving Ash feeling only slightly better than she had a moment ago.

She turned back toward the dock where the girls were already getting into the canoe. Michelle took a seat in the middle and then offered a hand to Tess, but Tess positioned herself at the very front of the canoe, wobbling only slightly as she settled in. Ash shook her head at the teenager's choice. Tess obviously thought she'd occupied the power position in the boat. This was going to be a long trip.

Ash handed the last paddle to Michelle before lowering herself into the back of the canoe. She stretched her legs in front of her and realized she'd gotten a lot taller since the last time she'd paddled a canoe. She cast her mind back to childhood summers spent outdoors with friends. She'd never been big on canoeing, but she could appreciate the calming effect of the repetitive motions. Once she settled in she found a comfortable stroke that felt vaguely familiar to her. Relaxing her back against the tail of the vessel, she kept her elbows comfortable above the side of the hull.

"Ready?" she asked, dipping her paddle into the water.

"Sure," Michelle responded, putting her paddle in the water. Tess didn't respond verbally but did the same up front.

Untying the back rope from the dock, Ash pushed off, and they paddled slowly away from the beach area until they were in open water.

Lake Alliance was at least two or three miles around with a heavily wooded perimeter. An occasional breeze stirred the calm surface of the water, blurring the reflections of sky and brightly colored leaves. The air was chilly, perfect weather for jeans and sweatshirts, and the deep autumn nights had most likely dropped the water temperature significantly as well. It seemed as though summer had disappeared on them altogether now.

Up ahead, Mary and a couple of boys paddled smoothly along the shoreline.

"Where do you want to head?" Ash asked the girls. "We've got almost two hours, so we can explore a little."

"Why don't we find some of those spots your new friend was talking about back there?" Tess suggested casually.

Ash refused to take the bait. "What do you think, Michelle?"

"I'm cool with whatever," she answered with her usual, easygoing attitude.

"Let's head for the far side of the lake, then," Ash said, dragging her paddle to rudder them in that direction.

They paddled in silence for a while, each getting the hang of their strokes. Ash and Michelle established a rhythm quickly, taking five or six short easy strokes on one side before shifting to the other. Tess, on the other hand, fought the paddle up front, gripping it like a baseball bat and sinking it as low into the water as she could, thrusting it out at a diagonal angle. Ash smiled at her attempts to throw her whole body into the stroke and debated whether or not to let her continue.

"Tess, if you put one hand on the top of your paddle and keep the other closer to the canoe it would be a lot easier," she finally called up to her.

"I can paddle a canoe," the girl shot back.

"It's up to you," Ash said with a shrug.

A few more minutes passed, and Ash noticed that Tess was pulling her strokes in closer to the boat in gradual increments, trying not to make it obvious that she was taking Ash's advice. By the time they were halfway across the lake, she had adopted a more comfortable position and Ash was beginning to relax into the repetitive movements. The day was absolutely beautiful. The fall temperatures hovered in the low sixties with a gentle breeze and not a cloud in the sky. While she had never been very big on the great outdoors, Ash had to admit that there was something appealing about the serenity of their surroundings.

Then again, maybe she'd gotten ahead of herself. Despite her even stroke, the canoe was drifting off course. Ash fishtailed her paddle in a J-shape away from the canoe slightly at the end of each stroke to hold them on track. As the canoe began to head back toward the opposite shoreline, Tess dug in more with her paddle on the right side of the canoe and Ash realized the girl was attempting to control the direction they were headed. She scanned the trees and rocks along the shoreline and couldn't see anything or anyone of significance, but still Tess kept pulling them hard in that direction, so Ash decided to let her go with it and paddled along with her. Tess promptly settled her paddle on the other side of the canoe and began turning them away.

It dawned on Ash that Tess wasn't interested in getting to a specific place on the lake, she was simply trying to figure out how she could control the canoe. She played around with different paddle strokes, slowing them down, speeding them up, turning left, then right. Ash wasn't sure why it mattered to her, but after a while she couldn't resist using her own paddle to counteract Tess's. When Tess pulled right, Ash went left just enough to keep them moving directly forward. Tess then switched left and Ash moved to the right, keeping them steadily on track. She had to fight a chuckle when Tess dug in powerfully to speed them up and she only had to give a slow, flat back stroke to slow them almost to a stop.

At this point Michelle turned around and looked at Ash, finally aware of the power struggle taking place. Ash quietly raised an index finger to her lips, signaling for Michelle to remain quiet. Tess, on the other hand, was either oblivious or attempting to seem that way as she fought even harder to make the canoe bend to her will. Eventually Ash grew bored with the game and raised her effort level. Now she wasn't just keeping the boat on track while Tess tried to pull them astray, she began actively steering them, using powerful draw stokes on either side of the canoe. She was in good physical condition, which made it hard for Tess to compete with her. The teen soon tired from her exertion and was only able to fight briefly before giving in. Slowly, she pulled her paddle all the way back into the boat and began to massage her bicep with her free hand.

"What's the matter?" Ash asked her sarcastically. "Need a break?"

"No." Tess pouted. "We're almost to the other side. I thought we should stop."

"Oh." Ash suppressed a grin.

"We've been at this forever." Tess sighed, pretending to be bored with the whole experience.

"Yeah, I guess it is getting late. You want to pick up the pace a little on the way back?" Ash prodded.

Tess turned around to look at her. When she did, the shift in weight sent them rocking.

"Whoa." Michelle grabbed the sides of the canoe.

"Careful, Tess," Ash warned.

"I'm not going to tip us," Tess said firmly.

"If you move around like that you just might," Ash shot back. She was losing patience with the stubborn teenager. Their outing could have been relaxing and enjoyable for everyone if Tess hadn't decided to turn it into a conflict.

"Hey, it's starting to get chilly," Michelle said. "Why don't we head back while we still have time to take it slowly."

Ash calmed herself with a deep breath. "That's probably a good idea."

"Fine," Tess quipped. "If you can't keep up, we'll slow down."

Ash clenched her jaw. "Tess, I'm in control of this canoe."

"What—because you're super dyke?" Tess glared at her.

"No."

"Because you're playing chaperone this weekend?"

Ash shook her head.

"Then why?" Tess practically spat.

"Because I'm sitting in the back, and whoever sits in the back of the canoe steers. So you can give up your little power play, because you can't control a canoe from the front seat."

Making her point forcefully, she turned the canoe around. She could tell from Tess's posture that she was seething, but she did not say a word as they began paddling. Ash unclenched her jaw and willed the muscles in her back to loosen. She had no idea why Tess got on her nerves so badly. Whatever the games, she was just a teenager and Ash tried to put her behavior in context. Tess could act out as much as she pleased, but in the end, she still wouldn't get what she wanted, if she even knew what that was. Ash didn't intend to be drawn into her dramas.

By the time they came close to the docks, she felt okay about how she'd controlled the situation out on the lake. Maybe all Tess needed was for someone to stand up to her. Ash decided to mention her strategy to Carrie and Mary. They allowed Tess to get away with far too much. She glanced toward her best friend. Mary and her group had climbed out of their canoe and were milling around the picnic tables with the hikers.

Ash steadied the canoe as Michelle tossed her paddle up, then pulled herself onto the dock. She reached down for Tess's paddle and offered her a hand. Ash was surprised to see Tess take it. She had a split second to wonder if maybe the girl had had a change of heart. Then it happened.

As Tess stepped up onto the dock she gave a quick, firm push-off with her foot directly on the edge of the canoe. Ash knew she was going overboard, but there wasn't a thing she could do to stop herself. She watched helplessly as the side of the canoe tipped into the lake and she had no choice but to roll with it. The cold water hit her like a slap in the face and immediately soaked her. She sank quickly to the bottom and immediately reacted by pushing herself back up. She broke the surface a few feet away from the dock, frigid cold shocking her entire body.

"Shit!" she shouted and started swimming.

Everybody ran toward her at once.

"Oh, my God," she heard Mary cry out as she was dragged from the water.

"Somebody get some towels," Carrie yelled.

Ash tried to pull herself to her feet, but she was shaking so violently she only made it to her knees. She was drenched. Her coat, her jeans, her boots: everything was dripping wet.

"Get her jacket off." Mary sprang into action.

Before Ash knew it people were stripping her clothes away. "Stop!" she yelled, pushing the hands aside. "I can do it myself."

She pulled off her jacket and stood up. Her teeth were still chattering and she couldn't stop shaking, but she forced everyone else to take a step back. When she did, she saw Tess standing at the end of the dock. Ash had to summon every ounce of control not to blow her top.

"What the hell, Tess?" she demanded.

"It was an accident." The girl shrugged, but she couldn't manage to wipe the smug look off her face.

"Oh, Tess, you didn't?" Carrie said, horrified.

In that moment, everyone seemed to realize that Tess had dunked Ash on purpose. Their angry stares only made Tess more self-satisfied.

With mock innocence, she told Ash, "I thought you said no one can control a canoe from the front."

"Mind if I join you?" Carrie asked, pulling back Ash's tent flap early that evening before Erin and Kevin could invade.

"Sure." Ash scooted over to make room.

Carrie took a seat next to her and held out a sweatshirt and a pair of shoes. "I thought you might like to borrow these."

"Thanks." Ash took them and placed them next to her.

"The shoes are Michael's. Apparently he brought several pairs."

"Ah, leave it to a gay man to pack a suitcase full of shoes."

Carrie smiled. "Well, it's not all Kenneth Cole. The sweatshirt is mine. I'm not sure it'll fit, but it's better than nothing."

"I'm sure it'll be great." Ash seemed touched. "You really didn't have to do that."

"I feel partially responsible for what happened," Carrie admitted.

She'd panicked when she saw Ash go into the lake. She held her breath until she surfaced again, but the relief she felt was short-lived. Ash was obviously freezing, and while Tess probably hadn't realized the danger in a prank like that, Carrie certainly did.

"You were nowhere near that canoe," Ash said.

"Yes, but I should have warned you."

"You knew Tess was planning on giving me a cold bath?"

Carrie laughed. "No, but I know what she can be like when someone makes her mad."

"Oh, so you thought you should have told me that Tess has a temper and that I have the uncanny ability to set it off, just in case I hadn't noticed?"

"Something like that."

"Well, that wouldn't exactly have been a news flash, now would it?"

"I guess not." Carrie wondered how Ash could be so good-natured about everything. It was times like this that made her second-guess her impression of Ash. Her understanding and sense of humor didn't mesh with her reputation as self-centered.

"So, are you still having a good time?" Carrie asked.

"I am now." Ash moved a little closer. "There's just one thing that would make this better."

"Ashton…" Carrie didn't finish her thought. She felt a shiver run down her spine.

Ash leaned in and her lips lightly brushed against Carrie's. It was just an instant, a split second of contact that set every nerve of her body tingling.

"We can't." Carrie pulled away. She heard a soft moan of protest.

"Why?"

"It's just not wise."

"Wise?"

"Yes. It would be too complicated." She struggled to remind herself why—her dean, her students, the tenure committee—anything to take her mind off the way Ash made her feel. Her breathing came heavily and her cheeks felt warm.

"It doesn't have to be." Ash leaned in again.

Carrie drew back farther, looking in Ash's eyes briefly before shaking her head. "It would be for me." Resolutely, she started to get up.

"Carrie, wait." Ash kicked her sleeping bag out of the way. "Don't go."

Carrie stopped just as her hand reached the zipper of the tent.

"I'm sorry, okay? Just stay."

Carrie hesitated. She could hear something outside the tent. Some of the teenagers were talking and from the sound of it, Tess was once again asserting her independence.

"What is it?" Ash asked.

"Shh." Carrie placed a finger to her mouth. She moved back toward Ash and they both listened.

"I don't care what she says," Tess announced. "She can rant about homosexuals all she wants. It doesn't matter to me. I do what I want to do."

"How did you get your mom to let you come with us this weekend?" one of the boys asked.

"Oh, I just lied and said we'd be back in time for church on Sunday." Tess laughed.

Carrie gasped. She couldn't believe Tess had put her in this position. Her mother would have her head over something like this. Before Ash could stop her, she bolted from the tent and marched over to the kids.

"Tess, please tell me you didn't lie to your mother," she said.

Tess tried to shrug off the question. "I had to get out of that house for a weekend. You know how it is."

Carrie ran her hands through her hair and exhaled forcefully, trying to calm herself. "I can't believe you did this."

"She can't do anything about it now," Tess answered defiantly.

"You don't get it, do you?" Carrie responded. "We're already walking a thin line. It's taken years for me to build up enough trust with her to let me bring you to these functions. When you do something like this, you undermine all of that."

"Like I said, I had to get out of the house."

The reply was so casual and Tess's attitude so patronizing that Carrie lost her temper. "Well, I hope you've enjoyed every minute, because it's probably the last time. And since you'd rather drown people who give up their time so you can have fun, I'm sure that won't bother you too much."

Without waiting for a reply, she strode away. She couldn't believe how Tess had betrayed her. It was the first time she'd taken the brunt of the girl's defiance. Even when Tess had lashed out at everyone else around her, she'd been willing to listen to Carrie. Now she was slipping further from her reach every day. She had to find a way to get through to her before it was too late.

When Ash caught up with her, Carrie had fought off her tears and was making plans. They would have to go back to town first thing in the morning.

"Do you think her mother would care if she missed church?" Ash asked. "I had the impression there's not much of a home life."

"Yes, she'll care," Carrie said. "You don't know this woman. She's as stubborn as Tess but without her sense of humor."

"What do you think she'll do if Tess isn't home until tomorrow afternoon?"

"I honestly have no idea. Sometimes she's in a forgiving mood, but other times she'll go on fire-and-brimstone rants that could shake the roof. I'm not going to take a chance on her calling the police and reporting Tess missing."

"You think she'd go that far?" Ash looked incredulous.

"I think she'd love to have an excuse to call us a bunch of homosexual predators who kidnap teenage girls."

"Can't you call her and tell her what happened?"

Carrie knew that was probably the right thing to do, but she hesitated to arm Tess's mother with any more ammunition. "I worry about what it would mean for Tess. I mean, her mother certainly knows she has a tendency to rebel, but still I think she would blame us for making her worse."

"And that would be the end of Tess's involvement with the center?"

"Very likely."

"Well, I hate to say it, but maybe that would teach her a lesson. She got herself into this mess. Why shouldn't she have to face the consequences?"

"There will be consequences," Carrie said. "I'm going to take her home first thing in the morning."

"How are you going to do that? You two rode out here with me."

"This isn't your problem. Don't worry about it. I'll talk to Mary and we'll figure something out."

"I know what Mary will say." Ash sounded impatient. "She'll pack everyone up and we'll all have to head back."

Carrie hesitated. She knew Mary well enough to know Ash was probably right. And the car shortage was a problem. She wasn't sure how she was going to handle the situation, but she didn't want to involve Ash. She'd put up with enough from Tess already.

"I'll take you home," Ash said abruptly. "If we leave at dawn, Tess can make it to church. You can deliver her to her mother, just as she expects. Then everyone else can stay here, enjoy themselves, and come home as planned."

"Why?" Carrie asked. "Tess has been nothing short of awful to you. Why do you care what happens?"

Ash met her eyes and something shifted in the depth of her gaze. The look was strangely tender. "Because you do."

CHAPTER TEN

I'm surprised we never met before," Ash said.

They stood in Mary and Sharon's driveway, watching Tess and Michelle load their stuff into Carrie's car. Tess had been quieter than Ash expected on the way back. She guessed the teen was probably dreading what awaited her at home. The thought gave her less satisfaction than she'd expected.

"I don't have much of a social life," Carrie said. "Everything is about work."

"Still, it's strange that we've never crossed paths."

Ash suspected from her conversation with Mary that there was a reason she'd never set eyes on Carrie before. Mary and Carrie had known each other for two years. Mary must have avoided inviting them both to the same events. She obviously thought Carrie deserved better than a one-night stand. Ash was starting to agree.

"I guess we just don't run in the same circles," Carrie replied.

Ash wondered if there was more to the comment than what was actually said. Was it that Carrie had a Ph.D. and Ash had barely finished high school? Or did it have to do with Ash's reputation? Either way, she couldn't think of a throwaway response. The truth was, both alternatives bothered her.

"Thanks again for bringing us home," Carrie said.

"Not a problem," Ash said.

"Well, you didn't have to, and it was a big help."

They stood there looking at each other as if neither wanted to say good-bye but they couldn't think of anything else to say.

"Do you have any plans for the rest of the day?" Ash asked.

"I should probably look at some of my students' papers."

"Oh, yeah." Ash nodded dumbly.

"So I'll see you later?"

Something in Carrie's face registered with Ash. She looked expectant, almost hopeful. Ash had seen that expression before, many times on the faces of many women. Except that in Carrie's case she wasn't sure what it meant.

Unsettled, she asked, "Wednesday, right?"

Carrie paused for a second as if trying to remember why they would see each other on Wednesday. Not exactly brimming with enthusiasm, she said, "Right, the bookcases. Yes, I'll see you then."

"Great." Ash got back in the car, silently cursing her own awkwardness.

What was she thinking? Why ask what Carrie was doing later and then drop the subject? She'd wanted to ask Carrie out, maybe to dinner or a movie. She didn't even know what she had in mind, now that she thought about it. She didn't know how to date, and she wanted to keep it that way. Whatever was going on with her, she wanted it to stop.

Ash fired up the Mustang and turned on the radio. Bruce Springsteen was singing "Born To Run," and Ash smiled at the serendipity of the moment. She was born to run, and she liked that. She rolled down the windows, turned up the volume, and sang along as she drove as fast as she could through the sleepy streets of Roosevelt. Drowning out her own thoughts in the noise of the radio, wind, and engine, she convinced herself that she just needed to clear her head. If she found something entertaining to do for the rest of the day and then got a good night's sleep, she would be back to her old self in no time at all.

❖

Carrie sat staring mindlessly out the window of her home office. She wasn't sure how long she'd been spacing out, but she wasn't getting any work done. Judging by the sun's position low on the horizon, she had let the entire day slip away from her unproductively. This bothered her. Normally she lost herself easily in her work and loved planning her lectures for the week, anticipating questions and imagining new ways to connect the course material to students' lives. Today everything seemed dull, and try as she might, she couldn't keep from thinking about Ash. They'd spent such a companionable ride home, and Ash seemed so sincere in her desire to help resolve the Tess problem, Carrie had thought how nice it would be to get to know her better. There was obviously more to her than met the eye.

Sure, Ash oozed sexuality. She was stunning, charismatic, and she made Carrie's body react in ways she'd never experienced before, but there was more than just physical appeal to her. When she let down her guard, Carrie really liked what she saw, a sweetness, a sense of humor, at times she even seemed sensitive, but she just hadn't had a chance to see it often due to the limited nature of their interactions so far. Carrie began to think that maybe she had been too quick to judge her. Tess had been nothing but awful to her, yet Ash had shown she could rise above petty retaliation. Before they went their separate ways, Carrie was certain Ash was about to ask her out. Yet she'd withdrawn before making the invitation. Carrie wondered why.

Puzzled, and slightly hurt, she foraged in her briefcase for the business card she'd kept there since Ash agreed to build the bookcase for her. The address on the card she extracted was downtown, probably a workshop of some kind, although it included an apartment number.

Carrie knew she was taking a risk as she got in her car and headed toward the older part of town. There was no guarantee that

Ash would be at home, if it was her home address. Still, she wasn't getting anything done and if she left it too late, she wouldn't go at all. As she wound through the narrow streets of storefronts and warehouses, Carrie wondered what she was even going to say to Ash if she was home. Ask her out to dinner? Coffee? It wasn't as if she could just say she wanted a real conversation to find out if Ash had a good personality.

She turned a corner just in time to see Ash's Mustang pull away from the curb in front of her apartment. Carrie slowed down, uncertain what to do. Ash had other plans, so she should just go home. She was already bordering on desperate by coming all this way in the first place and she never gave in to crazy impulses like this one. But instead of turning around, Carrie found herself following the Mustang all the way to the Triangle Club.

Carrie had never been in the club, but she knew it was the only lesbian bar in town. She also had a pretty good idea what she would find there. A lot of booze, a lot of smoke, and a lot of women. Ash would likely be right at home in those surroundings, but they certainly weren't Carrie's cup of tea. She shook her head, aware that she was judging again. Just because Ash was at a bar on a Sunday evening didn't mean her intentions were bad. Maybe she was meeting someone. That thought didn't make Carrie feel any better.

This is ridiculous, she thought. She was a grown woman. Why was she acting like this? If she wanted to talk to Ash, all she had to do was go inside and say hello. People had conversations in bars all the time. On the other hand, if she didn't want to go into the bar, then all she had to do was go home. No one was making her stay. Either way, she couldn't sit out in the parking lot all night wondering what Ash was doing and who she was talking to. That would just be pathetic.

❖

Ash walked into the bar and paused for a moment to let her eyes adjust to the dim light. The place was relatively empty. In one corner, a softball team sat around a table sharing pitchers of beer. They were carrying on loudly about their big win earlier in the afternoon. A few women were shooting pool at the back of the bar. There was no one on the dance floor. It was too early for the college crowd to be in, but that would change in the next few hours. As usual, Lupe was behind the bar.

Ash took a seat and waited for her to finish drying a glass.

"You're here early," Lupe said as she walked over. "You trying to make up for the time you missed the past few days?"

"Nothing escapes you, does it?"

"You think I don't notice when the local heartthrob goes missing on Friday and Saturday?"

"I didn't know you cared so much about me."

"Don't flatter yourself, chica." Lupe chuckled. "I care about my bar, and you just happen to be good for business."

"Then how about a Bud Light on the house?"

"How about a Bud Light that you pay for?"

"That'll work, too," Ash said. She liked the familiar banter with Lupe. It was comfortable. There were no double meanings or subtle hints. What you saw was what you got.

Lupe had just set down the beer when Ash felt someone settle onto the stool beside her. "I'll have the same, please."

The voice belonged to a trim brunette dressed casually in jeans and a white long-sleeved polo. She looked to be in her early thirties, very well kept, and neither completely butch nor femme.

"Put that on my tab," Ash said when Lupe returned with the beer.

"Thank you." The woman gave a brief smile of acknowledgment and extended her hand. "I'm Jeanette."

"Nice to meet you." Ash gave her name and took Jeanette's hand in a firm squeeze, which Jeanette demurely returned. Ash wondered briefly why women did that. Hadn't anyone ever taught them to shake hands? It wasn't supposed to be such a one-sided affair.

She focused her attention back on the woman in front of her. What did she care how a stranger shook her hand? It wasn't like her to notice something as insignificant as that. Jeanette was far from unattractive. She had curves in all the right places and a pleasant smile. No, this one certainly wasn't hard to look at.

"I've been working all day. I just couldn't take another minute in that office," Jeanette said, trying to spark up a conversation.

Ash adjusted her position so their bodies were closer together. "What line of work are you in?"

"I'm a realtor. Had a major open house this morning and I spent all afternoon trying to process all the follow-up requests."

Ash feigned interest. "Sounds like a good day."

"Sure, good for the bank account, but boring as hell. I could use a little something to spice up what's left of my weekend, if you know what I mean."

"I might." Ash knew exactly what she meant. Wasn't she here for the same reason? Jeanette was giving her all the right signals. All she had to do now was close the deal.

"I'm sure you do, sweetheart." Jeanette gave her a smile that seemed genuine but there was a hardness to it, like it didn't quite reach her eyes.

They were hazel, Ash noticed, and her gaze was calculating. She had the feeling Jeanette was already comparing her with other women in the bar, trying to decide who was worth her time. As Jeanette downed the remainder of her beer and signaled for another, Ash looked at the bottle in her own hand. It was still mostly full. She wasn't a lightweight, and she had never had any problem with women who drank, but the alcohol wasn't very appealing to her tonight. In fact, nothing seemed very appealing to her at the moment. Maybe she had settled too soon.

Without making it obvious that she was cruising her other possibilities, Ash scanned the other women in the bar. No one caught her eye. Some of the softball players were cute, but she wouldn't call any of them sexy. When she looked more closely, she recognized various faces and realized she'd slept with at least a third of the team. That was odd. They didn't seem all that attractive. Ash reasoned that the unflattering uniforms were probably turning her off.

One of the women shooting pool was a past bed partner as well. She was relatively attractive at first glance, but nothing special now that Ash was looking at her a little harder. Were her standards really that low, or was she just having an off night? She'd never been this picky before. She enjoyed women of all ages, races, and body types. She could usually get turned on at the drop of a hat. Why the sudden change?

She looked more intently at Jeanette. She was the most attractive prospect in the room, but Ash wasn't able to muster any enthusiasm over her. Jeanette's hand claimed Ash's leg. She was practically throwing herself at her.

"I'm ready to go, Ash. You want to head out and see if we can't find something better to do?"

Yes, Ash thought. *Just say yes.* This was her turf, familiar territory. She needed to get back to her routine. She needed to feel like herself again and this woman was offering her the chance to do that. She was attractive, available, and willing to let Ash take the lead. What more could she ask for?

"No thanks," Ash said, mentally kicking herself even as the words left her mouth.

"What?" Jeanette seemed surprised.

"I appreciate the offer, but I think I'm going to call it a night." Ash felt bad for misleading her, so she tried to give a charming smile. "If you wait till I finish my beer, I'll walk you out."

Jeanette shrugged, never breaking the contact between them. "If that's all you have to offer, then I guess I'll take what I can get."

❖

Carrie stood in the doorway watching the scene unfold before her. It had taken her almost fifteen minutes to work up the nerve to step inside the bar, and she now wished she'd gone home. Ash hadn't wasted any time. The brunette on the bar stool next to her was well into her personal space, and while Carrie couldn't hear them, the conversation appeared to be anything but casual. The woman's hand rested high up on Ash's thigh. There was something both suggestive and possessive in the touch that made Carrie's stomach churn with jealousåy. She knew she should leave. She shouldn't have followed Ash here in the first place. Everyone had warned her about Ash's reputation. Carrie wasn't sure why she needed to see the proof for herself. She truly believed people could change, but they had to want to. Ash had given her no indication that she was dissatisfied with her life. This was what she wanted, meaningless encounters and one-night stands. That's all this woman would be to her. She wouldn't even remember her a few days from now.

Carrie felt unreasonably angry as she watched Ash with the woman. She could only imagine what they were saying. Ash was probably turning on her trademark charm. Maybe she was even telling her some of the same things she'd told Carrie. Did she casually let her know how good she was with her hands? Was she telling the woman that she wanted her? Or was she simply making that fact known through the innuendo that came so easily to her? Carrie felt sick just watching them.

But why? Ash wasn't hers. In fact, she'd made it abundantly clear all weekend that she didn't want a physical relationship with Ash. So why shouldn't she find satisfaction with someone who shared her philosophy? Plenty of women would love a shot at someone so suave and attractive. She was sexy and charming, and everything anyone would want in a lover, but did any of them see beyond that? Did they know how sweet she could be? Did they ever look past the bravado and see that underlying vulnerability Carrie knew existed just below the surface? Would the brunette even stop to wonder who Ash was, what she cared about, what made her tick?

Carrie watched as the woman moved her hand up Ash's body and rested it gently on her arm. Would she ever know the pride Ash took in her work or realize how good she was with kids, or care about her the way Carrie did?

Her head spun with the realization of what she was thinking. She cared for Ash. She had feelings for her. Not just as an acquaintance, or even as a friend. Despite her best efforts and most fervent denials, she was falling for Ashton Clarke.

Carrie wanted to move, but her legs failed to comply. Ash and the brunette stood, the woman's hand still resting on Ash's arm. As they turned toward the door, Ash froze, looking directly at Carrie. Their eyes locked for a long, painful moment. Carrie read so many emotions flash across Ash's face, surprise, guilt, remorse. Still, the only thing she could process was the fact that Ash was about to leave the bar with another woman. It was a thought she just couldn't handle, so she turned and fled.

Chapter Eleven

Ash stood outside the coffee house watching Betty Ryan approach. When she saw Ash, she broke into a smile, weaving her way purposefully against the grain of the foot traffic on the sidewalk. Ash stuffed her hands in her pockets and watched her. She hoped she'd have half the fire Betty possessed when she was her age.

Smiling broadly, she held open the restaurant door as Betty reached her side. The place was filled with the usual weekday lunch crowd, students grabbing a bite to eat between classes and downtown businesspeople stopping in for a lunch away from the office. Ash settled in across from Betty at a small table in the middle of the room.

"They have a great peanut soup here," Betty said.

"Sounds good." Ash was starting to read her menu when the waitress approached them.

She looked familiar. Her long red hair was pulled back in a messy bun held by a pencil. She had gray eyes, a great smile, and legs a person would love to die tangled in. These looked great in form-fitting black slacks and she wore a white shirt with the top two buttons undone.

"Ash." She seemed happy to see her. "How are you doing?"

"I'm doing great. How are you, Shea?"

"Oh, things have been busy here, but other than that, I'm good."

Ash breathed a silent sigh of relief that she'd remembered the woman's name. "Good to hear."

"I've been meaning to call you."

"Yeah?" Ash started to get a little uncomfortable.

"I need a tune-up." Shea smiled playfully. "I mean my car needs a tune-up."

"Well, I'd be happy to take a look for you. If I can't fix it, I'll be able to send you to someone who can."

"I'm sure you'll be able to handle it."

"I'll have a water," Betty cut in.

Shea looked at her like she'd just appeared out of nowhere. "Okay, two waters coming right up."

"Who was that?" Betty asked as soon as they were alone.

Ash pretended to be absorbed in her menu. "Some girl I met a while back."

"She seemed pretty friendly to be just some girl."

"Betty, you know I'm too classy to kiss and tell."

"I think you did more than kiss her."

Ash just smiled.

"You just can't help yourself, can you?" Betty noted.

"What?"

"Oh, don't play coy with me. That charm of yours just comes natural. Women fall right into your lap without you even having to work at it."

Ash chuckled. "I wish that were always the case."

"When is it not the case?"

Carrie's face flashed across Ash's memory. Carrie breaking off the kiss, Carrie eating a toasted marshmallow. Carrie drying her hair, saying good-bye, standing in the doorway of the bar two nights ago looking heartbroken.

Shea returned with their glasses of water and took their order. After she walked away, Ash moved the conversation to more neutral ground. "So, Betty, what did you do on the weekend?"

"Same as always. Red Hat Ladies tea on Saturday afternoon, mass Sunday morning, soup kitchen on Sunday afternoon," Betty answered, sounding bored. "And yesterday I delivered meals to shut-ins from our church."

"You stay pretty busy."

"Not busy enough, if you ask me. After raising two kids and hauling them to catechism, marching band, football practice, and dance recitals, nothing seems very busy."

"But you have clubs of your own these days, don't you? What about the League of Women Voters?"

Betty waved her off. "You can only register so many people to vote in an off year before you end up just sitting around staring at each other."

"Is that why you resorted to learning to change flat tires?"

"Damn right! You get bored enough and you'll do anything. Even go to lunch with scoundrels like you."

"I thought you liked scoundrels." Ash pretended to be offended.

"Oh, I like a good cad as much as the next woman, but it's just not the same as having someone to fuss after."

"I thought that's what you were doing here," Ash teased. "Aren't you going to fuss after me?"

Betty laughed. "It's not that you couldn't use some fussing, that's for sure, but somehow I think you have women lined up around the block for that job."

"None as enticing as you," Ash said with exaggerated charm.

"See? What did I tell you? You just can't help yourself."

They were both still laughing when their food arrived.

"Don't think I didn't notice that you switched the subject earlier from your personal life to mine," Betty said.

"I did nothing of the sort." Ash sampled the peanut soup. The initial taste was exactly what she expected, creamy and slightly sweet, but as she swallowed, the heat began to spread across her tongue accompanied by a slow burn. "That's hot!"

Betty gave her a puzzled look. "Well, blow on it."

"No." Ash took a drink of her water. "I mean it's spicy."

Betty shook her head. "First the artillery punch, now the soup. You really are a lightweight, aren't you?"

"I just wasn't expecting it, that's all." Ash braced herself and took another spoonful.

"You were changing the subject again, is what you were doing," Betty insisted. "It's your turn now. What did you do on the weekend?"

"I went camping."

Betty regarded her suspiciously. "You don't strike me as the camping type."

Ash chuckled. "Usually I'm not, but a friend needed help chaperoning a youth trip."

"You definitely don't seem like the chaperoning type."

"Yeah, well, they were desperate."

"So, is this friend the woman you have your eye on?" Betty asked.

"No, this friend is happily partnered up and has a two-year-old daughter."

"So what's up with the one you're after?"

"She was there." Ash tried to sound casual.

"And?" Betty waggled her eyebrows.

"Well, apart from getting dunked in a freezing cold lake, I guess you could say it was an interesting trip."

Betty burst out laughing. "How did the dunking happen? Did you get fresh with her?"

Ash finished a mouthful of soup. "No, one of the teenagers did it. I wouldn't mind if I never saw that girl again in my life. She's a pain, but…" Ash sighed. "For some reason she's important to Carrie."

"And Carrie's important to you?"

"Yeah, well. I mean, I guess I like her."

"I have a hard time believing you'd put up with camping, dunking, and a hellion, all for some woman you just *like*."

Put that way, Ash could see her point.

Betty wasn't done. "You wouldn't spend a weekend at a youth camp for our waitress, would you?"

"For Shea? No."

"Then why this woman?"

"I don't know." Ash thought about the question for a moment. "Carrie's different."

"Are you in love with her?"

Ash choked and hastily lifted her napkin to her mouth. "What? No." She coughed again. "I mean, I'm not that kind of person. I'm not real big on love."

Betty looked at her, wide-eyed. "Settle down. I didn't mean to send you into a spell."

Ash took a deep breath. "I was just caught off guard."

"I can see that."

"If you knew me, you'd know how funny that question was."

"Because you're not real big on love?"

"Yeah."

"Then you'd better be careful," Betty warned.

"Why?"

"Because I think it might be sneaking up on you."

Carrie pulled the budget papers off her desk. "I'll get out of your way," she said.

"No, don't go," Ash said. "I mean, you can stay. You won't be in my way."

She shed the jacket she was wearing, revealing the tight gray T-shirt underneath. Carrie allowed her gaze to travel over Ash's body. Her arms were toned and muscular, causing the short sleeves of her shirt to fit tightly over her biceps. The fabric was stretched tight against what appeared to be solid abs and a naturally sculpted torso. Ash's carpenter jeans hugged her hips like they were tailor made for her. Carrie felt conscious of her own rather dull attire, brown corduroy pants and a soft maroon sweater that fit just snugly enough to accentuate her curves but certainly didn't come across as provocative.

Trying to sound cool and professional, she said, "I appreciate your coming in to finish the bookcases."

"It's no problem." Ash moved her tool belt over by the bookcase. "I enjoy the woodwork. I'll be sad to see it end."

"Will you be finished today?" Carrie wasn't sure how she felt about that prospect. It would be better for both of them to stop these interactions since they obviously weren't leading to anything. But still, despite her simmering anger over the incident at the Triangle Club, the thought of not seeing Ash again upset her.

"I'll wrap up all the woodwork today," Ash said. "Then tomorrow I'll finish with a varnish to protect it. That should be about it."

"Well, thank you for taking the time. I know you probably have bigger jobs you could be doing right now."

"Carrie, there's no place I'd rather be," Ash said.

There was a long silence. Neither Carrie nor Ash seemed to know where to go from there. The office was small and suddenly filled with the unspoken. Carrie wanted to say something casual about seeing Ash picking up that brunette on Sunday night, but she knew any remark would sound accusatory. Who was she to comment on Ash's personal life? Ash was free to do whatever she wanted with whomever she chose.

"I guess I should get started," Ash said.

She got her cordless drill out of her tool belt and used its smallest bit to drill pilot holes in the pre-cut shelves. It took everything Carrie had in her to concentrate on the papers in front of her and avoid stealing glances as Ash worked. She made it through the drilling without so much as sneaking a peek, but when she stood up to take a look at Ash's progress, she was surprised to find Ash watching her.

The expression on her face made Carrie blush. Her eyes seemed to be darker, her pupils dilated, and there was no mistaking the desire she saw there. Ash stood up without breaking eye contact.

"I'm sorry." Carrie stood as well. "I'm distracting you."

"Yes, you are." Ash stepped closer. Her breathing was uneven.

"I should go," Carrie whispered, but instead she took the remaining step to bring them within arm's reach of each other.

Ash wasn't sure who closed the final distance between them, but it didn't seem to matter the minute Carrie's lips touched hers. The gentle caressing quickly gave way to a bruisingly passionate kiss, and, as she probed deeper, she clasped Carrie's hips to steady them both. Carrie's hands cupped her face, holding her where she was. Neither of them was any longer in control of her own actions. Ash was blinded by a hunger that consumed every corner of her mind and body. The need to touch and be touched was terrifying and thrilling all at once.

Ash barely knew which way was up. On one hand all she wanted was to make love with Carrie, right here in her office. On the other she was smart enough to realize that she was dangerously close to wanting a relationship. She'd known Carrie for two weeks, and her initial infatuation had not worn off, which meant it had lasted about ten days longer than Ash was used to. Maybe it was because Carrie had been so hard to get, and the thrill of the chase was still present. But even if sleeping with her was all Ash needed, she wasn't sure if Carrie would let that happen. Either way, three days apart had only heightened Ash's desire. She knew she should stop, but she couldn't.

They stumbled backward so that Carrie was resting against her desk. As the kiss continued, Ash allowed her hands to wander, slipping beneath Carrie's sweater. They both gasped as her fingertips touched bare skin. Ash knew she'd crossed a line and could no longer stop herself. The attraction between them was too strong to deny any longer. She lifted Carrie onto her desk and began to kiss along her neck. Somewhere in the distance she could hear doors opening and closing, people talking and moving around. She was aware that the noises were getting louder, but that made no impact as she worked her way from Carrie's earlobes to the hollow at the base of her neck.

"Ash," Carrie panted.

Ash moaned at the sound of her name on Carrie's lips.

"We have to stop," Carrie said between heavy breaths.

The words failed to register fully in Ash's mind. Carrie's arms were still wrapped around her and her fingers were tangled in Ash's hair.

"I have a class," Carrie tried to explain as she once again captured Ash's mouth in her own.

"Cancel it," Ash mumbled.

Carrie broke away slightly. "We can't do this."

"Yes, we can."

They kissed again, slipping back into each other's embrace.

"It's too complicated," Carrie protested weakly.

"It doesn't have to be," Ash said. "It could be so easy."

Carrie pushed her gently away. "You don't get it, do you?"

Ash looked at her for the first time since they had started kissing. Her hair was tousled, her face flushed, her lips red and swollen. She was absolutely irresistible. "All I get right now is how much I want you."

Carrie sighed. "If someone came looking for me right now and saw this, it could end my career."

Ash leaned in again. "If you give me a chance, I promise I'll make you completely forget about tenure."

Carrie slid off the desk and stepped to one side, breaking all contact between them. "I know you would. You almost did." She picked up her satchel and headed for the door, stopping to look at Ash for another second before shaking her head. "I just can't let that happen."

CHAPTER TWELVE

The bookcases began to come together before her very eyes. Ash threw herself into her work, making twice her normal progress in half the time. She didn't know whether to be mad at Carrie for slamming on the brakes or at herself for letting things get that far in the first place. She didn't know what to make of a kiss that had almost brought her to her knees. She didn't know whether she wanted to run after Carrie or run away from feelings that were scaring her to death.

On the other hand, she did know how to sand the boards so they fit together tightly. She knew how to drive a nail so it was perfectly flush with the wood, and she knew how to set a rhythm and stay with it so her muscles worked on autopilot. Her work was not complicated to her; it was steady and fulfilling. Ash liked the way everything had its place, and that if she only did what others had done for centuries before her, she would get the same satisfying rewards.

She put the finishing touches on the woodwork and started brushing the varnish steadily over the bookcase. She had no idea how long she had been working when she heard the door open behind her.

"Carrie?" she murmured.

"I can be whoever you want me to be" was the rude awakening from Tess, who stood smugly in the doorway with a backpack slung loosely over her shoulder. She wore a pair of navy blue dress slacks with a yellow Our Lady of Mercy High School polo that showed her midriff.

Ash groaned. Just when she thought the situation couldn't get any worse. "Don't you have a home to go to?" she asked through gritted teeth.

"No, but we could use your place." Tess batted her eyelashes.

"Go to hell."

Tess flopped down into Carrie's chair like she owned the office. "What are you doing here?"

"I'm building bookcases, what does it look like?"

"It looks like you were waiting on the edge of your seat for Carrie to come back from her classes."

Ash ran her hand distractedly through her hair. Was she that obvious? "Tess, I'm really not in the mood for this right now. I can go somewhere else. How long are you going to be here?"

"Until Carrie gets done with her classes. She takes me to catechism on Wednesday nights." Tess laughed sarcastically. "Want to hear sick humor? I spend all day at a Catholic school and then the one chance I get to be around another dyke is on my way to catechism."

"You? A Catholic?" Ash let herself chuckle at the thought. First Betty, now Tess. Ash thought that some members of her own family would faint at the notion of liberals and lesbians at mass.

"No." Tess spun the chair around so she was facing Ash. "I'm not Catholic. My mother is Catholic. I am Teresa Maria Donnelly, her dyke of a daughter, who needs to go to church seventeen times a week so I don't rot in hell."

Taken aback by the force of Tess's anger, Ash raised her hands in surrender. "Hey, kid, I'm sorry."

"You're not sorry, and I'm not a kid!" Tess stood up, grabbing her bag.

"Where are you going?"

"What the hell do you care?" With that Tess slammed past Ash, knocking her off balance long enough to get past.

Infuriated, Ash spun around and got a firm grip on the girl's upper arm, just under her shoulder. "What is wrong with you!"

"Fuck." Tess winced sharply and jerked away, clutching her shoulder as if Ash had stabbed her.

The reaction didn't seem phony. Ash reached for her, this time more carefully. "What's wrong? I barely touched you."

"Just leave me alone," Tess snapped.

Even as she spoke, Ash caught a glimpse of a nasty, deep purple and blue bruise high on her arm. A shiver ran up her spine. "I didn't do that."

"No shit."

"Let me see it, please." Ash took a closer look at what she could now make out as four separate bruises that had bled together, ringed in yellow and about finger-width apart. The marks had obviously been made when someone clutched Tess violently. Ash steadied herself and spoke slowly in attempt to keep her voice level. "Who did this?"

"I fell."

Ash touched Tess's other arm, pushing up her sleeve to reveal identical bruises on that shoulder. She fought against the mental image of how the bruises were inflicted. Subconsciously rubbing her own arms, she said, "Tess, I know what this is. Let me help you."

Ash felt sick to her stomach. She was trying to decide what to do when Carrie appeared in the doorway.

"Come on, Tess, we're running late" was all she said, without stepping fully inside and not even looking at Ash.

Tess didn't move. Anger blazed in her eyes and Ash knew she was being challenged. If she told Carrie, she would lose Tess's trust, if there was any. But if she kept her mouth shut, she risked Tess having to go through more than she already had.

Obviously sensing the tension between the two of them, Carrie rolled her eyes. "You two can't even be in the same room with each other, can you?"

Neither Ash nor Tess responded.

"Fine, it'll never happen again. I'm over it." Carrie sighed heavily. "Tess, let's go. Ash, just lock the door behind you when you leave."

"Carrie, wait. We need to talk." Ash realized she sounded pathetic.

"I'm sorry, but we're running late, and there's really nothing to talk about." The words sounded so detached.

Ash fumbled in her jeans pockets, pulling out her wallet and pushing another one of her business cards into Carrie's hand. "Please, just call me tonight, okay?"

Tess gave Ash a look that could have killed but said nothing.

"I'm going to be busy." Carrie headed through the door.

"It's important," Ash called after her.

"We'll see," Carrie said as she walked away.

Tess was silent most of the way to catechism. She usually sulked when headed for anything church related, but today she seemed resigned to attending. Quite frankly, Carrie was relieved. She wasn't in the mood to argue.

When she pulled into the parking lot of the church, she tried to force a smile. "Have a good class, Tess. Your mom will pick you up at seven."

"Don't call Ash," Tess said as she exited the car.

"What?" Carried tried to process the non sequitur.

"Just don't call Ash tonight," Tess repeated.

Carrie shook her head at the animosity she heard. Whatever Tess and Ash had been bickering about this time, the girl was still carrying it around with her. "Tess, just let it go."

"Fine." Tess shut the door and stalked off toward the church.

Carrie pulled out of the parking lot and headed home. Tess and Ash's argument was of little consequence to her now. Ash was obviously not role-model material. She'd made that clear time and time again. She had little regard for anything other than her own libido, and the list of character flaws didn't end there. She'd shown no respect for Carrie's wishes, and despite knowing how important Carrie's career was to her, she was willing to risk everything just to get laid. But then again, Ash wouldn't really be risking anything at all. Carrie would assume all the risk; *she* would be the one putting her reputation on the line. She was the one who would be heartbroken when she woke up alone and had to get used to being nothing but a one-night stand to a woman she had feelings for. Ash, however, could walk away and never think of her again.

When she thought about it in those terms, Carrie couldn't believe how easily she'd succumbed. She knew it was wrong to let her guard down, but Ash's charm was too strong for her to resist. Even after showering and changing clothes, she could still feel Ash's hands on her skin and hear her voice echoing through her ears. She'd been so lost in the moment that she'd almost allowed Ash to take her right there on her desk. She had crossed a line, and that scared her. She still wasn't sure how she had mustered the strength to stop, but she was certain of one thing. If they got that close again, she wouldn't be able to control herself.

No matter what she did around the house, she couldn't focus on anything but Ash. Images filled her mind, sweet moments, like those shared in Mary's kitchen, fused with memories of passionate embraces. The recollections of arguments and Ash's maddening disregard for the consequences did little to cool her down. Even seeing her with another woman at the bar hadn't cured the infatuation. What was it going to take to get her life back under control?

Carrie stood suddenly. Grabbing her car keys, she headed for the door. She wasn't going to be able to will Ash out of her mind or simply ignore the attraction. But she could think of one way to get Ash out of her system, one sure-fire way to make certain she walked out of her life for good. Carrie had been fighting her fascination for Ash long enough, and she was obviously losing. It was time to put an end to it right now, consequences be damned. Each moment spent with Ash carried greater risk than the one before. Sooner or later they would be found out, and when word got back to the dean, Carrie would lose everything she had worked so hard for. She had to get a grip on the situation, and fast. At least if she was the one who made the rules now, she would be able to end the relationship on her terms.

CHAPTER THIRTEEN

Ash didn't even finish staining the last few sections of the bookcases before calling it a day. She was entirely too distracted to keep working. Her head ached and she couldn't shake the sickening feeling in the pit of her stomach. As she drove home, her mind wandered through the events of the day. She couldn't help but feel that things had been in a downward spiral for the past two weeks. She could barely remember how she'd gotten involved with the whole mess in the first place. If only Mary hadn't talked her into a night at the youth center.

She wished Mary was at home, but recalled that she was at an educators' conference and wouldn't be home tonight until very late. Ash would have to handle everything on her own. By the time she turned onto her block, she had made up her mind to tell Carrie about Tess's bruises. She knew Tess would hate her, but if she was able to get out of a bad situation at home she would be better off in the long run. Maybe Carrie could even take her in.

As soon as the thought formed in her mind, Ash rejected it. If Tess was under Carrie's permanent care that would end any chance Ash had of winning Carrie over. She tried to convince herself that her life would be a whole lot easier without Carrie or Tess in it, but she knew her resolve would not be as strong if she were standing in Carrie's office. Her heart picked up speed as she had a momentary flashback of the two of them in each other's arms.

Ash shook away the image and began to climb the outside stairs to her loft. She'd only made it about halfway when she saw Carrie on the landing in front of her door, looking down at her. Ash had to fight to keep her composure. Her legs were weak as she took the final steps. Carrie was wearing blue jeans and a long-sleeved gray T-shirt. She looked wonderful in even the most mundane clothes.

"I don't know what to say," Ash blurted out. Her charms had failed her every time she'd been around Carrie. Why should this time be any different?

"Can we go inside?" Carrie asked.

"Sure. I mean, of course." Ash bumbled around and found her keys, then opened the door. "How did you know where I live?"

"You've given me several business cards. Your home address is the same as your work address." Carrie stepped inside, looking around the loft, the entirety of which could be seen from the doorway.

Ash followed her gaze to the kitchen directly to the right. A bar divided it from the living space, which Ash had set up as a workspace. Beyond that was Ash's bed, which was really just a mattress and box spring on the floor. She'd been meaning to make a real frame with a headboard but hadn't gotten around to it. In the far back corner was the only enclosure in the entire space. It housed a sink, a shower, and a washer/dryer combo.

The windows across the back wall looked out over the older area of downtown and had a view of several brick buildings. Ash had never really wondered what the place would look like to someone else since she rarely brought women home with her, but she now found herself wishing she kept it a little cleaner. She didn't know why, but she worried that Carrie would see it for the bachelor pad it was.

Carrie walked around, stepping over the spare parts and tools that were strewn around to a table Ash had built in the center of the room. She picked up one of the framed pictures Ash kept there and smiled. "This is you and Mary."

"Yeah." Ash smiled back. "That was right after we met."

"How long ago was that?"

"I guess it's been over ten years now." Sometimes it seemed like yesterday. Other times Ash felt that she'd somehow stayed as she was, but Mary had moved on.

"You look so young."

"We were. Would you like a drink?" Ash asked. "I've only got water and beer."

"Water would be great." Carrie continued to study the picture as Ash opened a bottle of water and carried it to over to her.

"It's hard to believe, really. I was only a little older than Tess is now when that was taken."

Carrie set the picture down and stared into Ash's eyes. "Let's not talk about Tess right now."

"Carrie…" Ash couldn't find the right words to start the conversation she was dreading.

Carrie took a few steps. Ash felt her heart beat faster as she followed her line of sight right to the bed. Carrie turned and looked at her. "You can't keep doing this to me."

"Doing what?" Ash's voice cracked on the words.

"Toying with me," Carrie answered flatly.

"Is that what you think I'm doing?" Ash was a little hurt that Carrie thought so poorly of her.

"What else am I supposed to think? You sweep in, all charming, acting so cute, and then when you get my guard down, you show up looking so sexy in your jeans and tight T-shirts with your muscles flexing and making a show of how good you are with your hands."

Ash was astonished and more than a little flattered. "I've been a bumbling idiot every time I've seen you, and you're the one dressed to the nines all the time. I'm sweaty and covered in sawdust. Just look at me."

"I am looking at you," Carrie replied. "I can't stop looking at you, or thinking about you, and it's not good for me. I am usually stronger than this, but you've gotten under my skin. I can't fight it anymore. You win."

"Carrie, I'm not trying to win anything." Ash's head spun as she struggled to understand yet another turn of events. "I want to do what's right for once."

"And for once I just want to do what I want." With that Carrie pulled Ash in and kissed her, a deep, passionate kiss that picked up where they had left off earlier.

Ash was caught off guard, but her instincts kicked in and she wrapped her arms around Carrie's waist, holding her closely. For just one fleeting moment, she questioned the wisdom of what they were doing. She needed to tell Carrie about Tess, but before she could finish her thought, Carrie slid Ash's tattered jacket off her shoulders and began tugging the T-shirt from her jeans.

Ash let out a moan. She wanted Carrie too badly to stop. Her lack of control was terrifying, but the feel of Carrie's hands running across the skin on her back was more than she could take. Any remaining doubts disappeared completely as her shirt dropped to the floor, exposing her from the waist up. When their eyes met, Ash saw the desire she'd suspected, and hoped, Carrie was hiding from her. She wondered if Carrie could see the same in her.

Gently, she ran her hands under Carrie's shirt and up the slender curves she'd admired from the first time she saw her. As the shirt came off, she took in the soft skin before kissing Carrie's neck and shoulders, breathing in her intoxicating scent. She reached around and deftly flipped the hooks on the back of her bra while sliding the straps from her shoulders. As the bra fell to the floor, Ash cupped the back of Carrie's head in her hand and laid her down softly on the bed.

She slipped off Carrie's shoes and kicked her own boots to the side before lying down beside her. Carrie reached over to cup Ash's face, pulling her back in for another deep kiss. This one was slower. The hunger was still there, the passion building. Their tongues intertwined through parted lips.

Carrie pulled Ash on top of her, and their bodies pressed together as the heat between them increased. Ash unhooked the buttons on Carrie's jeans and slipped them over her hips, along with her panties.

Looking down directly into Carrie's crystal blue eyes, Ash whispered, "You're so beautiful."

"Ash, you don't have to—"

"I mean it. You take my breath away."

Carrie held her gaze, but didn't say a word as she reached down and undid Ash's belt before popping open the button on the top of her jeans. Ash held her breath as Carrie slid the zipper down so slowly the tension was almost painful. Holding her body weight with one hand, Ash reached down with the other and helped push the loose-fitting jeans down over her hips.

With no more clothes to be removed, they turned their attention fully toward one another's bodies. Ash let more of her weight rest on Carrie, soaking up the feel of skin on skin. She slid one of her legs between Carrie's thighs, parting them as she did, and felt the heat that was building there. One more kiss and she bent her head lower and took one of Carrie's breasts gently between her lips, rolling her tongue over the nipple.

"Oh, God, Ash," Carrie moaned breathlessly.

Ash took that as a signal that she should continue, and gave the same treatment to the other breast as well. Carrie's hands slid through her hair, the nails sinking into the tender skin at the nape of Ash's neck. Their bodies rose and fell with each ragged breath, and Ash worked her free hand downward, caressing Carrie's smooth skin from rib cage to stomach, to hips, to inner thighs. As she got closer, she lifted her gaze to look directly into

Carrie's eyes. The passion she saw was overwhelming, and she was torn between the urge to look away from something so raw and personal, or to let herself drown in the depth of emotion. She was mesmerized and profoundly moved by the connection she felt for the woman beneath her. It was more than lust. She'd been in lust before, several times a week, usually. This was deeper and stronger, frightening and comforting all at once.

Ash was drawn back to reality by the sound of her name rolling off Carrie's lips. "Ash, don't make me wait."

The plea melted Ash's heart. This was what she'd wanted from the second they met. She had no desire to tease or show her own power; she simply wanted to give this woman whatever she wanted. So, with their eyes locked and her body hovering over Carrie's, she pushed her fingers inside, her thumb running expertly across Carrie's clit. Carrie immediately arched up to meet her hand and within seconds she lay shuddering in Ash's arms, waves of pleasure making her body quiver.

"Ash," she cried softly one more time before her body relaxed.

Shaking from the power of her feelings, Ash kissed her slowly and tenderly. "Are you okay?" she whispered after she had caught her breath. "Was *that* okay?"

Carrie propped herself up on an elbow. "That was amazing."

She smiled, sending Ash's heart beating rapidly again. She then inched closer for another kiss. Ash expected the tenderness of a cool-down kiss, but what she got instead was every bit as intense as the one they'd shared at the office earlier that day. She wondered how so much intensity could be sustained for so long, but as Carrie rolled her onto her back, she knew she was about to find out.

"It's been a long time since I've done anything like this," Carrie whispered, just before she lowered her mouth to Ash's.

The kiss was searching, reaching, causing a heat that started at Ash's lips and spread to the tips of her toes. She felt herself beginning to surrender, sinking further from control. She was so wrapped up in the woman on top of her that she barely noticed how open she was leaving herself.

As the kiss ended, she mumbled, "I don't think I've ever done anything like this."

Carrie paused, searching Ash's face for a moment, as if she were going to say something. Instead she bent her head and covered Ash's neck and shoulders in kisses, some soft and sweet, others longer and more intense. The kisses continued down over her collarbone, breasts, and stomach. Carrie traced the path her mouth took, lightly dragging her nails over skin still warm from her lips. She spread Ash's legs tentatively, then looked up, making eye contact. Ash felt a dull, unfamiliar ache in her chest and had to close her eyes briefly to steady herself.

Carrie rose up, never breaking the contact between their bodies. "Is this all right?" she asked softly.

"It's wonderful," Ash replied, finding the strength to gaze directly at the woman who was tenderly stroking her face.

They kissed again, slowing the pace, and Carrie moved her hands downward once more, this time in gentle, sweeping strokes.

Ash slid her fingers through the dark curls she'd longed to feel and breathed in the sweet scent that had become like a drug to her. She'd lusted after many women over the years, but she'd never been so swept up in anyone as she was with Carrie. The experience was utterly intoxicating. She was almost delirious, her heart racing at even the slightest touch.

Tucked neatly under Carrie, she lost herself in the sensation of soft hands caressing every inch of her body, stopping occasionally to give specific areas extra attention. At the same time she remained locked in a kiss that seemed never-ending. Carrie's tongue ran along her own, and they shared the same breath as their excitement reached fever pitch.

"Carrie." Ash gasped for breath, the exclamation sounding almost like a prayer as it left her lips.

"Are you ready?" Carrie whispered, her voice raspy from breathing heavily.

"Yes." Ash had never been more ready for anything in her life.

With one earth-shattering move, Carrie pressed her fingers between Ash's legs, sending shock waves through her. Ash found herself in sensory overload, her body screaming out in pleasure and her heart aching from an overwhelming sense of need. The yearning she felt was entirely foreign to her, and she became aware that she was clutching Carrie so tightly she no longer knew where her flesh ended and Carrie's began.

Eventually the shudders of pleasure weakened and then subsided, but she didn't move. Surprisingly she felt herself doing something she hadn't done for more than a decade: she drifted off to sleep with a woman in her arms. With Carrie's head resting on her shoulder, their breathing falling into time, and the sun setting through the windows behind them, she closed her eyes and gave in to the serenity of the moment.

Ash startled awake some time later. The sun had gone down outside, and it took a moment for her eyes to adjust to the lack of light in the loft. Through the groggy haze that follows a deep sleep, she could sense that something was wrong. Instinctively, she reached over to the other side of the bed and found only an empty tangle of sheets. Ash sat bolt upright and felt her heart begin to race. She flipped on the lamp next to the bed and frantically scanned the room until she saw Carrie sitting in one of the chairs in the living space.

She was bent over, slipping on the shoes Ash had thrown to the side when they fell into bed hours earlier. Ash felt a wave of relief rush through her when she realized Carrie was still there, still within view, but as things began to get clearer, her stomach turned over once again.

"Where are you going?" she asked.

Carrie stood up. Her makeup was completely gone and her hair needed to be brushed, but Ash had never seen her look more beautiful.

"I'm going home," Carrie answered flatly, not making eye contact. "I have a lot of work to get done tonight."

Ash's heart sank. She swung her feet around the edge of the bed and onto the cool wood floor, but she couldn't find the strength to stand up.

"Listen," Carrie said quietly. "I've never done anything like this before, and I'm not really sure how it all works."

"How what works?" Ash wondered if she would ever be around this woman without being completely confused by her actions.

"I mean, if we see each other around, do we just pretend this never happened?"

"Is that what you want?" Ash stood up and reached for her pants, suddenly feeling very cold and naked. How could Carrie pretend this had never happened?

"Yes." Carrie's voice wavered slightly. "I think that would probably be for the best. Don't you?"

"I don't even know what to say." Ash realized she feared Carrie walking out the door. The knowledge rolled through her, sparking anger.

"You don't have to say anything. I knew what I was getting into when I came over here tonight."

"Well, that makes one of us." Ash set her jaw, trying not to let her emotions get the best of her.

"Ash, don't make this any harder than it has to be. You got what you wanted and now I've gotten you out of my system. We can both move on."

"How do you know what I wanted? Don't I get to decide that?"

"I'm sorry, but your reputation precedes you."

"What's that supposed to mean?"

"It means you have one-night stands to get your fill of whatever it is you're after and then you disappear. No good-byes, no calls, no apologies, and absolutely no relationships."

Ash was silent. She had no retort because up until that moment, Carrie's description would have been dead-on. All she could do was stand there, staring at what she feared was the one exception to the rule. She felt herself begin to panic.

"Wait, please don't go."

Carrie paused. "Why? Give me one good reason why I should stay."

Ash made a desperate move toward her. "Did I do something wrong? I thought we—"

"Don't worry. This isn't about your competence. But you already knew that, didn't you?"

Bewildered, Ash said, "Don't you want more than just..." Words failed her. She didn't even know how to describe their lovemaking. She couldn't express the bond she felt between them, and she refused to accept that she was alone in her sense of deep connection.

Carrie swept her with a caustic gaze. "More than what?"

Ash felt like the walls of the loft were closing in on her, but rather than show her own weakness or admit her own need, she lashed out. "What about you, Dr. Fletcher?"

Ash called out, just before Carrie reached the door. "I bet I'm real convenient for you, aren't I? You can walk right out the door without a care in the world, because I have a track record. Well, what about you? When was the last time you had a relationship?"

It was Carrie's turn to stand and stare.

"Yeah, that's what I thought," Ash spat. "I want to have fun, you want to have tenure, and neither one of us lets anything get in the way of what we want, so don't judge me without looking in the mirror first."

Carrie took a few steps closer. "Ash, you can think whatever you want, but you're not in this for the fun."

"Oh no, Dr. Fletcher, do you have Ph.D. in psychology now, too?"

"It doesn't take a Ph.D. to know you want to be in control. All this is just a power trip for you, nothing more. I may be addicted to my career, but at least the work I am doing is for the greater good. You, on the other hand, are only in it for your ego." She paused, and a hint of sadness crept into her tone. "Well, count me out, Ash. You can add another notch to your bedpost over there, but that's the end of it. From now on, leave me alone."

With that, she walked out of the loft, slamming the door behind her.

CHAPTER FOURTEEN

Carrie tried to get her keys into the ignition but she couldn't see through the mist clouding her eyes. Exhaustion mixed with frustration and completely overwhelmed her. She rested her head on the steering wheel and allowed the tears to come. Sobs racked her body as she struggled to make sense of what had just occurred.

She had given Ash exactly what she wanted, and she had done so discreetly. She had avoided all chance of being caught and limited the risk to her career. Now Ash would disappear and she could get back to the tidy, orderly life she'd worked so hard to build. She'd accomplished everything she hoped for by visiting Ash. There was absolutely no reason for her to feel so despondent.

Yes, the sex was amazing, but it was just sex. Wasn't it? Carrie let out a groan as the images of her making love to Ash flooded her mind. She had expected the passion and the intensity, but the intimacy of the encounter had caught her off guard. She'd never felt so deeply connected to anyone before. She had been completely unprepared for the tenderness and sensitivity Ash had shown. Then there was the vulnerability she saw so clearly in Ash during their argument. Why hadn't Ash just let her go? It didn't make any sense. Ash had gotten what she was after, sex with no strings attached. Now she was free to move on to her next conquest.

Carrie took a deep breath and wiped away her tears. What was she doing sitting there worrying about Ash? It was over, that was all that mattered. Ash would move on, and now so could she. She could go back to working toward tenure without any distractions. Her life would return to purposeful and predictable normality. She had her dream job, the respect of her peers, and the admiration of her students. Wasn't that everything she needed?

Ash was left pacing in her loft. Drowning in her own thoughts, she wandered aimlessly around the confines of the apartment, which suddenly seemed much smaller than it ever had. Every direction she turned was filled with reminders of Carrie. It was almost like she was still present and Ash was bumping into her every time she turned around. She returned to her bed but couldn't bring herself to lie down. The sheets were still a tangled, lifeless mess without Carrie beneath them, and the pillows still smelled like those velvety curls Ash loved running her hands through.

She returned to the living room and set about reorganizing her toolbox, but no matter how hard she tried, she couldn't concentrate. Despite her best efforts to focus on the familiarity of her tools, all she could see was Carrie, sitting in the chair or standing at the table with the picture in her hands. She could still see Carrie smiling back at her and hear the echoes of their argument. Yet nothing could be worse than standing in the kitchen realizing she was alone. Ash wasn't sure if she'd ever acknowledged her loneliness as she did now.

In the past, she'd found ways to escape the feeling. She was almost always around other people. Or there was a woman in her bed. Or Mary was at the other end of the phone. If Ash didn't want to be alone, she could simply avoid it.

Ash walked over to the sink and attempted to occupy herself with the past week's worth of dirty dishes. She glanced at the door Carrie had slammed behind her when she had walked out. The silence there was deafening.

Ash had almost reached the breaking point when the phone rang. She practically dove across the loft, grabbing the receiver before it rang a second time. "Carrie?"

"Ash?"

"Mary." Ash's heart sank, but at the same time there was a slight sense of relief. She ached to hear from Carrie, but at least with Mary she knew where she stood.

"What's going on?" Mary asked cautiously.

"I thought you were out of town." Ash dodged the question, still shaken.

"I'm on my way home. I hadn't heard from you for a few days, I thought I'd check in." Mary's voice filled with concern. "What's happened?"

"I don't even know where to start." Ash hung her head, not wanting to rehash the entire scenario.

"Ash." Mary's voice was slow, her words measured and careful. "Are you okay?"

"Yes," Ash lied. "I mean, I'm not hurt or anything."

"What happened with Carrie?"

"How did you know?"

"Give me a break. Think about how you answered the phone."

Ash didn't reply. She couldn't even begin to put into words what had happened or what she was feeling.

"I tried to warn you," Mary continued. "I knew one of you was going to get hurt. That's what happened, isn't it? Sounds like you got burned this time."

"Mary, I don't know what's going on. It's all so messed up. Then to top it off, Tess is in trouble."

"What kind of trouble?" Mary perked up, obviously not expecting this addition to the story.

"I think it's her mother," Ash said, not finding the shift in subjects any more pleasant.

"Did you tell Carrie?"

"Tess won't let me, and Carrie doesn't want to hear anything from me right now. You have to get through to them."

"Ash, I'm still two hundred miles away. There's nothing I can do," Mary replied. "I'm sorry. You know I would love to bail you out, but you're on your own with this one."

"I told you I'm in over my head here." Ash felt herself giving in to both anger and frustration once again.

"Whose fault is that?"

"Mine," Ash answered angrily. "But I don't know what to do. Neither of them will talk to me."

"I love you, honey, you know that, but you've made your bed this time. Lord knows I tried to stop you, but you're going to have to grow up a little here and fix things."

"Mary, I was born grown up. Don't give me that."

"In some ways yes, but in other ways you've never had to face the consequences of your actions. Part of that is my fault for always bailing you out, and part of that comes from the fact that your charms are your own worst enemy. Either way, it's time to pay the piper."

"Fine." Ash resigned herself to her third lecture of the day. "Then just tell me what I need to do, and I'll do it."

"I can't tell you that, Ash." Mary's voice softened. She sounded like a mother who'd gone from giving a scolding to relating the moral of the story. "If you really think about it, I'm sure you'll know what needs to be done."

"I don't even know what I'm feeling anymore."

"It's love, honey. You're in love."

Ash could sense a smile in the voice on the other end of the line.

"I don't do love." Her throat tightened at the mere mention of the word.

"Fine, then be your usual stubborn self. Screw up your life

once again if that's what you want to do, but don't come crying to me afterward." The outburst was followed by nothing but a dial tone.

Ash stood dumbfounded, staring at the phone in her hand. She couldn't believe Mary had hung up on her. *What's wrong with these women?* she thought.

She felt like the whole world was shifting around her and she was the only one managing to stand steady. In less than twelve hours she'd felt the highest of highs and the lowest of lows. She had been yelled at by a teenager she was trying to help, a woman she was trying to please, and a friend who had been her rock for over ten years. Now she couldn't even find peace in her own home. Was nothing sacred anymore?

She had to get out and clear her head. She needed to go someplace safe, someplace familiar, someplace that hadn't been changed by the whirlwind she'd survived. She grabbed her jacket from the floor and the keys to the Mustang off the counter. She knew just the place.

Ash could feel the dull thud of the bass shaking the floor and rumbling through her core from where she stood in the doorway of the bar. The lights were low and the music provided a loud rhythm that flooded out into the street. The Triangle Club wasn't as crowded on a Wednesday as it would be on the weekend, but even from where she was standing she could see the friendly face of Lupe, the bartender, already waiting for her order.

"Ah." Ash breathed in deeply, smelling a distinct mix of cigarette smoke, sweat, and pheromones. "It's good to know some things never change."

As she wove her way across the dance floor, a few women turned and looked. One of them, a bold little brunette, placed a hand on Ash's shoulder, a move Ash shrugged off. She gave the woman what she hoped was a not-too-confrontational glare.

Perhaps, she admitted to herself, some things were different, even here. Any other night, she would have at least stopped and given the women a good looking over before she made her way to the bar, but tonight anybody other than Carrie was going to fall short of her standards. Besides, she wasn't here for a fling, she was here for a drink.

Ash took a seat at one of the tall stools facing the bar. She was glad to find that there was no one sitting directly on either side of her. The last thing she wanted was to have to make polite conversation with someone she wasn't the least bit interested in. The soft butch tending bar walked over to her.

"What, no cute little Latina nicknames for me tonight?"

"Sorry," Ash replied, "my Spanish is limited."

"That's never stopped you before,"

"*Una tequila*," Ash said. "How's that?"

"That'll work." Lupe cast an uncertain glance at her, as if she didn't know what to make of her resident Casanova's mood swing.

"Make it a double," Ash called as the bartender walked toward the bottle of Cuervo.

She took the time to look around. The usual group of hardcore party girls controlled the dance floor. No matter what night Ash came in, they always seemed to be there, bumping and grinding to whatever the DJ had to spin. Sometimes she wondered if they slept there when the music stopped and hopped right back up again when it started once more. Farther back in an area cordoned off by another half bar, a group of more butchy women were shooting pool and playing darts. The area was usually filled with women in various stages of groping and undress who took refuge in the leather couches provided for just those types of encounters. Tonight, however, appeared to be sports night, and Ash didn't think the butches were likely to give up their pool table anytime soon. Just as well, she thought. She was in no mood to make any trips to the couches tonight.

"Here ya go." Lupe had returned with her drink.

Ash sat there staring at the double shot for a few seconds before lifting it to her lips and tossing her head back. The warm liquid immediately spread its heat throughout her mouth, and she held it there for a second before she swallowed hard. The burning began as soon as the liquid hit her throat, and worked itself all the way into her stomach before spreading out through her entire body. Ash rolled her head and felt her neck and back muscles start to unwind. She had never been a heavy drinker, but she was beginning to understand why other people gave in to the urge.

"Hey, there's some little chick making eyes at you from the end of the bar," Lupe whispered slyly.

Ash didn't even look up. "Not tonight, I've got a date with another tequila tonight." She slapped her shot glass back onto the bar.

"I've never seen you turn down a sure thing before." Lupe looked confused. "Chica, if it were anyone else, I would say you'd found yourself some girl trouble in a big way."

"Well, if you mean all the women in my life have suddenly gone crazy, then I guess you could say I've got girl trouble."

The bartender laughed, a deep, hearty laugh. "I never thought I'd live to see the day. Who is the lucky lady?"

"There's no lucky lady." Ash sulked. "Just a few things out of whack. Nothing a few days rest and little more tequila won't fix."

"You know," Lupe filled Ash's glass, "I've been pouring this stuff since, well, probably before you were born, and I have never once seen it fix a single problem."

Ash groaned. "No more lectures. I can't take another person giving me a heart-to-heart about my bad behavior."

"Not a lecture, just an observation." With that she placed a glass of water next to Ash's tequila.

Ash looked at her accusingly, but before she had a chance to say anything, Lupe raised her hands palms upward in mock surrender and walked off to greet another customer.

Ash paused just a moment before picking up the shot and

tossing it back. She swallowed the second it hit the back of her throat, but instead of burning, this one simply felt warm on the way down. Either the first drink had dulled her senses or the bartender had poured her a little less this time around. Ash figured it was probably a combination of the two. She reached for the water, sipping it gingerly as if it were the drink that had made her head feel lighter, and not the tequila. At least now she was starting to loosen up. The music didn't seem as loud or as harsh as it had when she came in. The occasional patron brushing up against her wasn't as annoying. And most of all, the dull ache in her wasn't weighing on her mind nearly as bad as it had been half an hour ago.

"Ay, *papi*," the bartender exclaimed, walking back over to Ash. "Take a look at that."

Ash turned around on her stool and followed her line of sight toward the door. It took a minute to get a clear view, but when she did the tequila seemed to instantaneously lose its grip on her. Standing in the doorway was quite an impressive figure, dressed in a short white skirt and a skintight black top, her blond hair loose and streaming down her back. Ash felt her entire body tighten with dread.

It was Tess.

She looked defiantly at Ash, as if daring her to blow the whistle, but when Ash didn't move, she turned away and disappeared onto the dance floor.

"Damn her," Ash mumbled.

"She's quite the piece of work."

Ash just eyed the bartender. "She's trouble."

"You oughta know."

"Just gimme another drink."

Lupe reached under the bar and pulled out a Bud Light, twisting off the cap.

Ash raised her eyebrow. "I was drinking tequila."

"You were. Now you're drinking Bud. Got it?"

There was no questioning the statement. Ash was peeved,

but she was afraid she would get told to go home if she shot off her mouth, and the only thing waiting at home for her was the memory of Carrie.

"Now come on." The bartender leaned forward. "What's the story on the chica?"

"She's just a kid. She shouldn't even be in here. She's only sixteen."

"Yeah? And how old were you the first time you lied your way into this bar?"

Ash shook her head. "That's different."

"Right, because the rules don't apply to you, just the people around you?"

"Yes. No. Son of a bitch, I'm not in the mood for this," Ash almost shouted, setting her beer down on the bar so forcefully that some of it spilled out onto her hand.

"Settle down," Lupe said gently. "I know you've had a bad day, but it looks like she has, too."

Ash glanced at Tess, who was dancing halfheartedly with a college student. She had to admit, Tess certainly didn't look like she was there for kicks.

"Now, my bet is that she wouldn't be here if she felt like she could be anywhere else, so I'm going to do the same thing for her that I did for you and plenty of others through the years."

"What's that?" Ash asked.

"I'm going to look the other way and let her spend an evening away from whatever it is she can't handle at home."

Ash thought about it for a moment. If Tess were forced to leave, God only knew where she would go. "Fine, let her stay. I've been told several times that she's none of my business, so I'll just keep out of it."

With that she returned to her beer, while at the same time trying to keep an eye on where Tess was and who she was with. She couldn't help but remember her own teenage trips into dyke bars. She'd fought, she'd smoked, she'd drunk anything she could get her hands on, and she'd started going home with any woman who caught her eye. She cringed at the thought of Tess getting drunk or high and following some woman wherever she led.

Ash wondered why this bothered her so badly. She'd survived, hadn't she? She had turned out okay. With the exception of the past two weeks, she'd been very happy, so what was wrong with Tess learning some life lessons young? Lupe was right: judging by the bruises Ash had seen earlier, Tess was probably better off in a bar than she was at home. Still, Ash couldn't shake the feeling that they were both headed for a disaster.

Ash got so lost in her own thoughts that she didn't know how much time had passed since she'd seen Tess. The bar had gotten busier, and it was harder to see everyone on the dance floor. Ash scanned the dark room and tried not to panic when she couldn't see Tess. Surely she would have noticed if she'd left with someone.

"Lupe," she shouted at the bartender, who was taking drink orders at the other end of the bar, "where's Tess?"

"Who?" Lupe, yelled over the music.

"Tess! The girl that shouldn't be in here."

Lupe rolled her eyes. "She was shooting pool last time I noticed."

Ash quickly looked over to the pool tables, and sure enough there was Tess perched on the edge of a table, chatting up some young dyke in a leather jacket. They were each holding a pool cue, but it looked like the game had come to a halt as Tess said something and she and the young butch threw back their heads laughing. The butch stepped up and slipped her arm around the small of Tess's back under the pretense of being worried that she was going to fall off the edge of the table.

"Oh, that was smooth." Ash snorted.

"Settle down." Lupe flicked her with a bar towel. "She doesn't seem to mind."

"She doesn't know any better." Ash took a swing of her Bud, which seemed awfully flat after the tequila.

"Boy, you got it bad for this kid, huh?"

"What?" Ash choked, sputtering beer all over both of them.

Lupe laughed. "She's got you all worked up, chica. She's awful young to be brooding over, don't you think?"

"It's not like that," Ash grumbled.

"Oh no? What's it like, then?"

"She's headed down a dead end." Ash tried not to think about what that meant for her, since Tess seemed to be doing exactly what she had done.

"Hey, what doesn't kill you makes you stronger, right?" The bartender shrugged.

It might not kill her, Ash thought, *but it will definitely kill Carrie.*

She returned her gaze to the pool area when she heard a dull thud. The young butch held Tess against the wall.

Ash wasn't exactly sure what happened, but something inside her snapped. She didn't know if she was thinking about how scared Tess must be, or what something like this would do to Carrie, or remembering herself at that age being kicked around some dark barroom. Before she had time to fully form a plan, she bolted from her stool and hurdled the bar between her and the pool area. She grabbed the butch by the back of her neck and pulled her off Tess.

She caught a look at Tess's eyes. They were filled with a deadly mix of anger and terror, but she barely had time to process the stare when a fist caught her cheek, just above the corner of her mouth. The blow knocked her off balance and she had to stumble to keep from sprawling across the floor. The rusty taste of blood spread through her mouth, accompanied by a dull throb. She clutched the side of her face automatically and felt a trickle of blood spread across her fingers.

Groaning, Ash drew herself back up and squared off to face the butch again. For the first time she really looked at her opponent. She was about twenty-one, maybe slightly older, and it was obvious she thought of herself as a tough guy. She was just an inch or two shorter than Ash, with coal-black hair cut short and spiked. Her build was solid and she had dark, angry eyes offset by the burning red handprint across her face. Tess must have slapped her for something.

Ash could tell that this one had a temper and was incapable of letting a slap slide. Her pride had been wounded and she wouldn't care who she took it out on as long as someone was made to pay. The whole scenario seemed all too familiar to Ash. In fact, if she hadn't known better, she could have been convinced that she was looking at herself seven or eight years ago.

She studied Tess and realized that if someone didn't stop her now, the terrified girl against the wall was going to turn into the kind of angry woman Ash knew well. So would the young butch who stood in front of her, with fists raised and eyes blazing, angry at the world. From there they would probably evolve into the type of selfish, apathetic person Ash had become, a woman incapable of trusting anyone enough to open up fully. The realization sent her reeling more than the punch had. Her head spun as the pieces of the puzzle all began to fall into place. Was this what people saw when they looked at her?

The butch moved toward her again quickly, striking out with another punch. Luckily Ash saw this one coming and was able to block it with her forearm in time to throw a punch of her own. The blow landed across the side of the butch's mouth, and Ash felt her knuckles crack as they made contact. It had been several years since she'd hit anyone and she grimaced at the sickening feeling it gave her. Her stomach turned as the butch went down, landing on her back. Ash looked closer and saw blood oozing from a tear in the woman's lip.

Not wanting things to go any further, she grabbed Tess around the waist and started edging her toward the exit, all the while keeping her eyes on the young butch who was cupping the side of her face. When she started to stand up and raise her fists once again, Ash just shook her head. "She's sixteen."

"She's what?" The butch dropped her fists, stunned.

"She's only sixteen. Let her go," Ash said flatly.

The butch, obviously not wanting to draw any more attention to herself than she already had, took a step back and raised her hands. "I'm sorry, I didn't know. She said she—"

"Yeah, I know." Ash took Tess by the arm and started walking. "Are you okay?"

"I'm fine, and I didn't need—"

"Yeah, I got it, but now it's time to go home."

"I can't go home."

Ash stood and thought for a moment. "Me, either," she admitted, but then looked around at the bar. "But we can't stay here, either. Let's go for a walk."

Tess seemed leery but was willing to let herself be led. Ash grabbed her coat off the stool and tossed some money to Lupe, who just nodded as they passed by the bar and headed out onto the street.

Ash and Tess started walking without another word between them. The night was cold and dark, but the streetlights were enough to compensate for the cloud-covered moon. They passed bars and restaurants, closed-up store windows, and dark offices. Ash wasn't sure where they were headed as they cut a random pattern across the neighborhood, and she didn't really care. It felt good to be moving away from the noise and smoke of the bar. Even though her head was still spinning from the realizations that had literally punched her in the face, at least outside she could think clearly.

She glanced over at Tess, who was matching her pace with long, determined strides. Ash realized the girl was probably feeling even more lost than she was. The anger that had radiated from her earlier was now gone, supplanted by a look of fear. Ash noticed her shiver slightly, and without a word she slipped off her coat and extended it toward her. Tess touched the jacket like it was a foreign object, then she expanded her gaze to take in Ash, as well.

"I can't go home," she said flatly, like she was thinking out loud, or more likely repeating a mantra that had been running through her head since she said it in the club earlier, maybe even before that.

"I know." Ash slipped the jacket over Tess's shoulders. "I can't, either, not yet."

"No, you don't understand, I can't go home, ever." The statement could have come across as overly dramatic, but given the situation it seemed to just be a statement of fact.

"Tess, I meant what I said earlier. I want to help you."

"You can't." The pouting, sulking tone Ash had come to expect from her was absent. This time Tess's voice was filled with desperation.

"Why not?" Ash asked softly. Normally she would have been sure she could handle anything, but after everything that had happened in the past twenty-four hours, she wasn't sure of anything anymore.

"My mother is determined to save my soul, and I can't take another day of it."

"Those marks on your shoulder, those are supposed to save you?" Ash felt anger welling up inside her.

Tess snorted. "Yeah, she'd like to shake the gay right out of me."

"Tess, you don't have to stay there. I know Carrie would take you in."

Tess dismissed the idea quickly, and Ash realized she was probably not the first person to think of it. "Mother would never let me live with another lesbian."

"Screw her." Ash raised her voice. "She hurts you, she doesn't get a say. We'll call a social worker."

"She'll turn me over to Catholic family services rather than let someone outside of the church take me. Would you like to go live in a Catholic home for troubled dykes? You want to sign yourself up for some reparative therapy bullshit?"

"What's the alternative? You can't go home, you can't live with anyone other than the Catholics, so what can you do?"

"You're looking at it." Tess looked down at herself and then back toward the bar.

"No, that's not an option, either." Ash was adamant about that; she knew now that she couldn't let Tess go down that road.

"Why not? It worked for you, didn't it?" Tess was trying to muster up some of that defiance she usually hid behind, but Ash could see through it now.

"You can do better than I did."

"Better? Is this a pep talk? Is that what you think I need right now?" Tess was next to tears.

"It's not a pep talk, it's the truth. You can do better than I did, but not if you go back into that bar. If you go back there, you're going to turn into another hard, lonely kid just like I was."

"So what's wrong with that? When was the last time someone hurt you?"

Ash caught her hand. "Today."

"Yeah, right."

They started walking again.

After a while, Ash said, "Tess, I was stubborn and independent, but that didn't keep me from being hurt. I'm going to tell you something I've never told anyone." She took a deep breath. "A long time ago I lost the woman I loved because I was so busy trying not to get hurt that I didn't even realize I was in love with her. She found a great woman, and they've built the perfect life. I missed out, and I've kept missing out ever since then. Hell, just today I did it again without even meaning to. Don't let yourself turn out like that."

Tess slowed down. Looking into Ash's eyes, she said, "I don't know how not to. Do you?"

Ash thought carefully. "A gay-friendly Catholic home that would be willing to take in a feisty young lesbian?"

Tess nodded. Her eyes were red and puffy from crying, and the night wind blew her hair around.

"Actually"— Ash laughed in spite of the pitiful sight in front her—"I may know just the person to help out."

CHAPTER FIFTEEN

Ash slowed the car to almost an idle as she turned onto Mason. Large oak trees filtered the soft light of porch lamps and projected shadows onto the two-story homes that lined the street. She thought to herself that the neighborhood was probably very warm and welcoming under normal circumstances, but given the current situation its silence seemed tense and fragile. She knew Tess's house without even seeing the address. Light shone through every bay window on the lower level, illuminating first the pristine white porch and then tumbling out onto the perfectly manicured lawn, providing a bright contrast to the sleepy darkness of the surrounding homes.

"Mary's here," Ash said, a little surprised to see her friend's station wagon parked across the street.

Tess looked over blankly as though she were incapable of processing anything beyond the conflict that awaited her. "That's Carrie's house." Ash felt her heart skip a beat and her breath catch in her throat. Carrie was Tess's neighbor, how could she have forgotten that? She would have been the first suspect when Tess went missing. She and Mary were probably beside themselves right now, perhaps even sitting in there with Tess's mother.

As they stepped onto the porch, Ash saw the welcome mat in front of them and found it ironic since she was most certainly not going to be welcomed into the house. Before she could even process the thought fully, the front door swung open and a woman who could have been Tess's older sister stood in the doorway. She was younger than Ash had expected, probably only in her early forties. Her hair was long and blond like Tess's, her body was lean and trim with only minimal signs of gravity beginning to take its toll, and her eyes were the same piercing blue, but with none of the spark.

"Get your hand off my daughter" was all she said, in a tone so quiet and cold it sent a shiver down Ash's spine.

Ash didn't move. "Take a step back."

"I will not." The woman flinched slightly but remained planted in the doorway.

"Fine, we can do this on the front porch, then. I'm sure all your neighbors will be interested to hear you've been trying to beat your teenage daughter into submission."

A flash of anger flicked across the woman's face, then she looked past Ash with a frown.

"Tess!" Carrie rushed up the pathway. Mary was right behind her. "We've been so worried."

Chaos reigned for a moment as everyone spoke at once. Somehow they all ended up in Tess's living room. The interior was smaller than it looked from the hallway, or maybe it just felt that way. An entertainment center occupied the front of the room, and a couch sat behind a coffee table along the back wall. A recliner and another little end table sat in front of a large bay window on one side of the room, and the other side branched off into either a set of stairs or a long hallway. The only real decoration was a large crucifix that hung over the television. Ash wondered briefly what message that was supposed to convey to visitors.

"What happened to you?" Carrie touched Ash's cheek, sending a sting through the side of her face.

"That?" Ash had forgotten about the punch she'd taken only about an hour before. "That's a wake-up call."

Carrie looked at her quizzically. "Dare I ask what's going on?"

"It's obvious, isn't it?" Tess's mother snarled. "I should call the police and have you arrested."

Ash reached over to a portable phone sitting on an end table. "Go ahead, call the police." She took the receiver and thrust it in the woman's face. "While they're here, we can go ahead and show them the marks on your daughter's shoulders."

"What marks?" Carrie asked.

When Tess displayed the multicolored bruises, the color drained from Carrie's face, and she looked like she was going to be sick. "Oh, my God. Who did that to you?"

Tess didn't have time to say anything before her mother snapped, "Take your hands off her." To Ash, she spat, "The police won't believe a word you say. You're a dyke that's been out all night, God knows where, with a half-dressed teenage girl."

"That's ridiculous!" Ash was not comforted by the fact that, if asked, she'd have to admit she and Tess had been in a gay bar where she was drinking tequila and had gotten into a fistfight.

"Is it? How do I know you won't take advantage of her?"

"Take advantage of her?" Ash rolled her eyes. "Lady, I have absolutely no romantic interest in your daughter."

Tess's mother raked her with a cynical glare. "Just give me one reason why I should believe that."

"Because I'm in love with Carrie," Ash blurted out.

"What?" Carrie gasped.

"Oh, my God." Mary covered her mouth with both hands.

"That's not love, that's lust," Tess's mother said, disgusted.

Ash shook her head but kept her eyes locked on Carrie's. Neither of them knew what to do with the revelation. Everyone seemed frozen, time suspended, until the silence was broken by a knock at the door.

"Thank God." Ash rushed to the door, thankful to escape the dazed stares.

"Did you call me here at this ungodly hour to flirt or to help?" Betty asked as Ash showed her in.

Ash laughed for the first time that night. "You're here to save the day," she said. "Without further ado, I'd like you all to meet Betty Ryan."

"Good evening, Elizabeth." Betty greeted Tess's mother in a tone that suggested familiarity.

"Hello, Betty" came the guarded reply.

"You two know each other?" Ash asked, not sure whether or not that was a good thing.

"We attend the same church," Tess's mother answered, her mannerisms much more cautious than they'd been a few minutes prior.

"Well, I guess that will make this easier," Ash said.

"Make what easier?" Elizabeth cast a confused look toward Betty.

"To put it plainly"—Ash took a deep breath—"Tess will not be staying here."

Ash watched as Mary's taillights faded into the night. She finally willed herself to turn around and look at Carrie, afraid of what she might see. Carrie seemed stunned by the latest turn of events, or maybe she was simply reeling from Ash's unexpected confession. Their eyes met and Ash felt her knees go weak at the softness in Carrie's gaze.

"I don't know what to say," Carrie said, in almost a whisper.

"It's okay," Ash stepped closer. "I'll start." She took a deep breath before continuing. "I was a jerk today, and yesterday, too. Well," she fumbled for words, "I guess I was kind of a jerk over the weekend, and what I am really trying to say is, I'm sorry?"

"*You're* sorry?" Carrie seemed flabbergasted.

"Yeah, for the things I said earlier today, and for not telling you about Tess sooner and for, for everything really." She looked away, suddenly worried that her apologies were too little, too late.

"Ash." Carrie took her hand, sending a spark through her fingertips that made Ash have to stifle a gasp. "I'm the one who should be apologizing. You tried to tell me earlier, didn't you?" She covered her face with her hands. "The things I said to you, Ash. I'm so embarrassed."

Ash thought that Carrie was the most adorable thing she'd ever seen. She pulled her closer, holding her tight. "Carrie, I'm so glad you said it, all of it."

"How could you be?" Carrie buried her face in Ash's chest.

Ash reached down and gently tilted Carrie's chin upward until they made eye contact. "If you hadn't said it, I wouldn't be here right now."

With that she bent just enough that their lips met, gently at first. Ash felt her knees buckle at the tenderness of the kiss, but as the seconds passed she felt the familiar heat of their earlier encounters begin to rise. She held Carrie in her arms tighter as their lips parted, giving way to hungry mouths. It took all of the strength she had to pull away.

"We can't do this here," she said breathlessly.

Carrie blinked. They both seemed to have forgotten that they were still standing in the street in front of her house. "You're right." She blushed. "Let's go inside."

She took Ash's hand and cut across the yard and onto the porch. Ash followed blindly behind her, so closely that they almost collided when they got to Carrie's door.

Carrie turned the knob one way and then the other before, frustrated, she resorted to simply shaking it in a vain attempt to open it.

"The lock." Ash chuckled, burying her face in Carrie's neck and kissing the soft skin along the collar of her shirt.

"God." Carrie fumbled for the key. "Why do you always do this to me?" They stumbled through the doorway, laughing. "Do you think I'll ever learn?"

"Oh." Ash smiled broadly at the sound of Carrie's laughter. "I'm sure in time you'll get used to it."

Carrie paused and looked into Ash's eyes, her face illuminated by the streetlight shining through the open door. "Ash, you've got me on whatever terms you want me, but please don't talk about a future. It'll only get my hopes up." Then she leaned in again, pressing their lips together.

Ash's head spun. Had Carrie misunderstood? As their lips parted slightly Ash felt Carrie's tongue curl around her own. Her head was screaming at her to stop, but her body was crying out for something else. Carrie slid her hands up underneath her shirt. At the feeling of Carrie's skin against hers, Ash felt her body begin to take control of the situation. She moved her hands to the small of Carrie's back and lightly massaged the flesh beneath them. All the while the passion of their continued kiss increased.

Then out of nowhere, the image of Carrie walking out the door flooded Ash's mind, and she pulled away. "Carrie, wait." Every nerve in her body protested the interruption. "We should talk."

"Talk?" Carrie stepped dangerously close again.

"Yes, about where this is going."

"I thought this was going upstairs." Carrie began unbuttoning Ash's shirt.

"Dear God," Ash mumbled as she felt Carrie's warm mouth kissing the now-bare skin on her chest. "Please, Carrie, I'm only human," she said, summoning the remainder of her strength and pulling away one last time.

"You really want to talk?" Carrie asked, seeming slightly leery of Ash's intentions.

"Yes, I want to talk." Ash wasn't sure if she was trying to convince Carrie or herself.

"Okay." Carrie reached past her to switch on a table lamp.

Both women blinked and squinted as their eyes adjusted to the light that flooded the room. Ash looked around her. She should have known Carrie would have a perfect home. Soft colors filled the living room, from the cream-colored couch and love seat to the pale blue armchair in the corner. Everything said comfort. Everywhere Ash looked, there seemed to be books. They were spread out on the floor and the coffee table; they lined the walls in cases and in stacks. She hoped she would be around long enough to build bookcases for them all.

Carrie sat down on the couch and motioned for Ash to sit next to her. Ash moved toward her, but when she inhaled the sweet smell of Carrie's shampoo, she said, "I think I'd better stand. I don't seem to have much restraint when I get too close to you."

"Ash, what is it?"

"Carrie," she started slowly, not exactly sure how to put her feelings into words, "I haven't been in a real relationship in a long time, maybe not ever."

"I understand, and I'm not trying to change you," Carrie answered, looking her directly in the eye.

Ash couldn't help but smile. "I don't think you do understand."

"You've never misled me about what you want."

"I've misled *me* about what I want."

Carrie shook her head. "You need your freedom."

"That's what I thought, but I was wrong," Ash blurted out. "I need you."

"You have me." Carrie hid her face in her hands.

Ash crouched down so she was level with Carrie. Taking her hands away from her face and holding them in her own, she said, "Carrie, I want a relationship with you, and I am willing to go as slow as I need to go to prove that I love you."

When Carrie looked up, Ash saw tears in her eyes, and her

heart stopped. Did Carrie not feel the same way? Had she gone too far too fast?

"What is it?" she finally asked.

"I love you, too" was all Carrie managed to say before they lunged for each other once again.

CHAPTER SIXTEEN

Carrie reached up, cupping Ash's face in her hands and pulling her in closer, but when her fingers ran across the torn skin on Ash's cheek, they both winced. "I'm sorry." She drew back. "Did I hurt you?"

Ash smiled. "No," she replied honestly, "I've never felt better."

"You look awful."

"Gee, thanks."

"That's not what I meant." Carrie got flustered. "I was talking about the cut. It looks awful. You look…" Her eyes took in Ash, scanning her body from head to toe. "Amazing."

Ash felt a fire begin to burn just below the surface of her skin, and she started to step in for another kiss, but Carrie shook her head.

"We need to get something on that cut."

"It's not that bad." Ash pressed her lips to Carrie's. For a moment she felt Carrie give in, then a hand pressed against her chest and gently pushed her away.

"I can see you are going to be hard on my resolve, Ms. Clarke," Carrie said.

Ash smiled sheepishly but felt her knees weaken when Carrie's deep blue eyes met her own. "No, Dr. Fletcher, I'm afraid all the weakness is in me."

"I find that hard to believe."

"Me, too." Ash smiled.

Carrie pulled her in again, wrapping her arms around her waist and resting her head on Ash's shoulder. "It'll be our little secret," she whispered. "Now come on. Let's get some peroxide on that cut. I don't want any scars on that perfect face of yours."

When they reached the top of the stairs, Carrie led her into the bathroom and turned on the lights. Ash saw herself in the mirror and grimaced. The cut looked worse than it felt. There was a jagged tear, and the edges were turning various shades of deep blue and purple.

Carrie opened the medicine cabinet and pulled out a bottle of peroxide and some cotton balls. "Have a seat." She motioned to the toilet seat and Ash sat down. She was through arguing.

Carrie poured a liberal amount of peroxide on the cotton and gently dabbed it on Ash's cheek. Ash flinched when the cold liquid hit her open wound, but Carrie held her chin and blew softly on the bubbling cut.

Ash smiled at the sweetness of the gesture. "God, you smell good," she mumbled.

Carrie laughed softly, pouring more peroxide on a new cotton ball. "Flattery won't get you out of this." She leaned in again and pressed the cotton a little more firmly to the wound. Ash felt a stream of peroxide run down her neck and onto her shirt.

"It'll bleach your shirt. Take it off."

"What?" Ash laughed.

"Take off your shirt." Carrie grabbed at the bottom of the garment and pulled it over Ash's head in one swift move, leaving her sitting on the toilet seat bare-breasted.

"Hey!"

"I didn't want it to get ruined." Carrie offered an innocent smile.

"Sure." Ash hesitated just a moment before jumping up and grabbing her around the waist. Her vast amounts of practice at undressing women were too much for Carrie, who was too busy laughing to put up much of a fight. Her shirt came off in a matter of seconds, as did her bra, before Ash spun her around so their bare skin pressed together. They both had to take a moment to stop laughing before Ash could kiss her once again.

The instant passion of the kiss signaled that playtime was over and they had delayed the inevitable long enough. Without breaking the contact between their bodies or their lips, Ash walked Carrie backward out the door of the bathroom.

"Where's your bedroom?" she asked between ragged breaths.

Their mouths were back together again so quickly Carrie couldn't even answer, but she hooked a finger into one of the belt loops on Ash's jeans and guided her across the hallway. They continued through a doorway, clinging to each other on their way across the dark room until Carrie backed into her bed. She kicked off her shoes and fell onto the mattress, pulling Ash down on top of her.

"The light," Ash whispered, moving down to place kisses along Carrie's neck and jawline.

"What?"

"Is there a light?" Ash stopped for a second, hovering above Carrie. "I want to see you."

Carrie reached up and flipped the switch to a small reading lamp on the bedside table. The soft light was enough to illuminate the large four-poster bed and throw shadows across the rest of the room. Ash stared at the woman below her. She was breathtaking, and Ash suddenly felt nervous and unsure of herself. She had never cared so much about pleasing a woman. This was new territory and she was uncertain as to how she should start.

"I want to make love to you," she said.

Carrie nodded. "I want that, too."

Ash shifted onto her side, pulling Carrie close to her. She ran her hands over every inch of her exposed flesh while placing kisses gently on Carrie's lips, cheeks, and neck. Taking an earlobe between her teeth, she nibbled softly and felt Carrie exhale and clutch her tight. Ash smiled. She was going to love taking the time to learn what pleased the woman she'd fallen in love with. She had never been so turned on by the prospect of knowing every intimate detail of someone's body.

She moved lower on the bed so that her lips now dragged along Carrie's neck and shoulders. She kissed a path across each one of her collarbones while reaching down to unbutton Carrie's jeans. Carrie arched up, lifting her hips off the bed, so that Ash was able to slide them off completely, and when she did Ash returned her attention to the upper part of her body. She propped herself up directly over Carrie and lowered her head, running her tongue from one nipple to the other. She would circle each slowly, tantalizingly, until Carrie arched up to meet her fully.

Carrie moved a hand up Ash's back and neck, intertwining her fingers in her hair. She ran the fingers of her other hand just underneath the waistband of Ash's pants. She didn't move to unbutton them right away, just teased the skin until Ash could barely concentrate.

"Take them off," Ash urged in a hoarse whisper.

Carrie didn't hesitate. She flipped open the button with one hand and then slowly pulled the zipper all the way down. Without ever breaking the contact between them, she removed the pants and dropped them on the floor.

Ash let her body come to rest once more, this time without any barriers between them. She wanted to feel as much of her skin as possible touching Carrie's. She let her hands roam slowly over Carrie's body once again, moving farther south across the soft skin of her torso and stomach. She ran her fingers down Carrie's side and felt the solid muscle of her thighs. Not wanting to miss an inch, she reached even farther down, to caress Carrie's firm calves. She felt the muscle flex under her touch and wondered absently what kind of exercise produced such an exquisite figure.

She slowly worked her way back up Carrie's body, giving more attention to the inner side of her calves and thighs. She slid her hands upward, massaging gently as she went until she was close enough to feel Carrie's heat on the tips of her fingers. She was torn between the desire to continue exploring the body beneath her and the need for release, when she was suddenly hit with a realization. She didn't have to fit a lifetime's worth of exploration into one night. For the first time in her life, she actually had a lifetime to look forward to. If she'd dwelled on the gravity of the situation, it would have been overwhelming, but with Carrie's body calling out to her, she surrendered to the moment. Lowering her head, and feeling Carrie's fingers in her hair, she let herself be pulled into the body she'd been enjoying.

Carrie's passion had been building so steadily that upon contact she gasped sharply and clung to Ash. She responded to every stroke of Ash's tongue. Her breathing quickened, and her body arched in an attempt to increase the contact between them. Ash held nothing back, giving every ounce of energy to her lovemaking. She found herself so invested in Carrie's pleasure that she almost cried out when she felt Carrie's shivers of enjoyment grow into full-fledged convulsions. Every muscle in Carrie's body seemed to contract at once, and she released a deep moan. Her fingers dug into Ash's neck and shoulders, melding their bodies into one and holding them fused, until with a heavy exhalation, her muscles relaxed and she sank back into the mattress.

When her tremors subsided, Ash crawled up toward the pillow and collapsed onto the bed. She took Carrie's face in her hands and drew her in for a slow, gentle kiss.

"You're amazing," she said when she finally caught her breath.

"Me?" Carrie's eyes were wide in surprise. "You're the amazing one. I've never felt anything like that before."

"Me, either," Ash admitted, basking in the warmth of the afterglow.

"Oh no, you don't," Carrie laughed, propping herself up on her elbow. "No dozing off yet. I'm not done with you."

With that Carrie leaned over and kissed her, but it was certainly not a wind-down kiss. The passion between them quickly reignited every nerve ending in Ash's body. Her heart skipped a beat and she found herself looking up into the seemingly endless blue of Carrie's eyes.

Carrie smiled down at her, one of those smiles that melted her heart. "You are so beautiful," she whispered, running her finger down Ash's chest and tracing a lazy pattern around her breasts.

Ash blushed. She'd been told that she was good-looking, sexy, or hot, but beautiful? That seemed so personal. Did Carrie really see her like that? She didn't have to wait long for the answer. Carrie once again leaned down and pressed her lips to Ash's. The kiss was a deep, soul-searching kiss. Their lips parted and her tongue explored Ash's mouth while her fingertips continued their own survey of other parts of Ash's body. She felt Carrie's hand run over her shoulder and down her arms, squeezing her biceps gently as they went. She continued until their fingers met and became intertwined, then she lifted Ash's hand to her mouth, and breaking the contact between their lips, moved to sweetly kiss each one of Ash's fingertips. From there, her mouth and fingers once again parted ways. Her hand moved farther down Ash's body and her mouth worked its way back up along her arm, shoulder, and neck. When she reached the tender skin on Ash's neck she began to kiss, softly at first, then more firmly. The sensation sent goose bumps across Ash's body and a moan escaped her lips.

"Hmm." Carrie smiled. "You like that?"

"Yes," Ash gasped, her voice thick with desire. "You're a quick learner."

Carrie didn't respond. She just kept working her way around Ash's neck and down her other side, kissing and nibbling, occasionally running her tongue across sensitive areas. In the meantime her hands had moved down, grasping at Ash's hips, kneading the skin and pulling Ash's body toward her own. Ash arched up willingly, eager to feel Carrie's body pressed against her. Carrie's hands slipped under her, running across her back and down toward her legs. She continued to move down along the back of Ash's thighs, causing Ash's legs to spread, and she used the opportunity to let her body settle between them. At the same time the path of her kisses moved across Ash's stomach and down to her thighs.

Ash held her breath in anticipation, her heartbeat pounding in her ears. The suspense was almost painful, and she fought to maintain her composure, but when she felt Carrie's tongue on her, she gasped and had to clutch the sheets to steady herself. Her head swam and her body tingled with the overload of sensations. Carrie maintained a gentle pressure, continuing to caress any part of Ash's body within her reach. Ash felt her pleasure building, causing her to lose any semblance of control. With one final stroke Carrie sent her over the edge. Ash called out in ecstasy. Every one of her nerve endings felt raw and exposed, shaking under Carrie's skillful touch. To Ash it seemed that she'd never come down until slowly, gasping for breath, her body went limp.

Ash felt Carrie rest her head on her chest, her body nestled in the crook of her arm. As she closed her eyes and stroked Carrie's soft curls, the thought occurred to her that now was usually the time she'd begin plotting her escape, but tonight she couldn't move even if she wanted to. And she didn't.

"Can I stay here tonight?" she asked softly.

Carrie gave her one of those knee-weakening smiles. "You'd better."

They kissed softly. Their passion, quenched for the moment, had been replaced with tenderness.

"I love you," Ash whispered when Carrie's head was once again resting softly on her shoulder.

"I love you, too," Carrie replied.

❖

Ash woke up the next morning surrounded by the smell of Carrie. She opened her eyes slowly, afraid she'd been dreaming, but as her blurry vision came into focus she could make out the outline of the woman next to her. Carrie's soft curls were in disarray, cascading across the pillow and down her back. She lay on her side, the sinewy curves of her body covered loosely with a sheet. Her eyes were closed and the corners of her mouth turned upward ever so slightly. Ash's heart melted at the sight. She wanted to pull her close and kiss her, or wake her up again to tell her how beautiful she was, but she looked so peaceful it seemed wrong to disturb her.

Ash would have been content to lie in bed all morning just looking at the woman she loved, but the dull throb in her cheek warned her that she'd better take care of the cut on her face before the pain took hold. Trying to avoid sudden moves that might wake Carrie, she slipped out of bed and padded across the cold hardwood floor, picking up articles of her clothing along the way. She had no idea what time it was, but the amount of light that was streaming through the window was enough to tell her their exhaustion from the night before had made them sleep away most of the morning.

She checked her injured cheek in the bathroom mirror. The cut didn't seem as big as it had the night before, and thankfully it didn't look infected, probably because of the peroxide, but the skin around it had turned purple. Ash couldn't gauge the extent of the damage and decided that she'd better take something light to dull the pain. She paused for a moment, not sure whether or not it was appropriate for her to open the medicine cabinet; it didn't seem right to peek into someone's personal belongings without her knowledge. Then again, didn't people in relationships do that sort of thing? Having never been in a relationship, she wasn't sure how long it took to get to the stage where both parties would feel comfortable going through the other's cabinets and drawers. After thinking about it for a while, she decided to err on the side of caution and get some ice instead.

She made her way downstairs and through the living room to the kitchen. It was small but immaculately clean, with each utensil and small appliance in its appropriate place. Ash immediately thought of the contrast it offered to her own kitchen and shuddered before focusing her attention back on finding some ice. The clock on the wall told her it was after eleven, and she didn't want to allow the pain any more time to get settled in, but she couldn't help standing in front of the refrigerator for a moment, absorbing the unfamiliar domesticity of her situation. When in her life had she spent hours making love with a woman, then casually roamed her kitchen, fully intending to return to bed and pick up where she left off?

She took some ice from the freezer and wrapped it in a dish towel she found on the kitchen counter. Gingerly, she touched the bundle to her face and wandered back into the living room and sat down on the plush, cream-colored couch. She didn't want to turn on the TV for fear of waking Carrie, so she picked up a book off the coffee table. *Undoing Gender* by Judith Butler. Sitting back, she wrapped herself in a maroon afghan that was draped over the arm of the couch, opened the book, and began to read.

She didn't even make it through the first sentence before she got stuck. She wasn't sure she understood the individual words, and she certainly didn't understand them when they were used together. Ash scratched her head and read on. Things just got more complicated from there.

For the first time it really sank in that Carrie had a Ph.D. She apparently enjoyed reading things that Ash couldn't even begin to comprehend. Phrases like "normative personhood" were not in the day-to-day vocabulary of someone who built bookshelves and changed tires for a living.

Carrie awoke suddenly. Without opening her eyes she sensed that she was alone. Part of her knew she should have expected it.

Ash wasn't the kind of person who stuck around the morning after. Still, she was hurt. She had let herself believe that this time was going to be different. Ash had said she loved her, and she had shown it in so many ways in such a short time. Carrie didn't want to believe Ash might not have meant what she said.

She sat up slowly, trying to process all of the feelings that were beginning to overwhelm her. Something just didn't add up. Ash had chosen to profess her love; Carrie hadn't asked for it. She had offered herself completely on whatever terms Ash was comfortable. Why would Ash feel the need to pretend if there was obviously no pressure to do so?

Carrie wrapped herself in her robe as if the chill that had settled over her body could be warmed away. Her clothes from last night were still scattered across the floor. She glanced at them briefly but was in no mood to clean up. Then something caused her to take a second look. There, underneath her jeans, was one of Ash's boots. Carrie followed the path they had taken last night. There was a sock and then another boot. *Surely Ash wasn't in such a hurry to leave that she did so barefoot?* Carrie allowed herself a shimmer of hope as she made her way quickly down the stairs.

She let out a ragged sigh of relief when she saw Ash curled up on the couch.

Ash smiled up at her. "Good morning, beautiful."

"When I woke up and you weren't there…" Carrie started.

"You thought I left?"

Carrie nodded. "I guess part of me still can't believe that last night really happened and that you're still here."

Ash stood and took Carrie into her arms. "I'm here for as long as you'll have me."

"You do know that'll be a very long time, don't you?" Carrie asked, nuzzling closer and resting her head on Ash's chest.

"I hope so."

Carrie looked up, her relief giving way to curiosity. "What were you doing down here, anyway?"

"I was putting some ice on my cheek," Ash replied and picked up the bundle she'd set on the table when she had gotten up.

"Is it bothering you?"

"Just a little."

"Why didn't you take any aspirin?"

Ash shrugged sheepishly. "I'm kind of new to this relationship thing, and I don't know what the rules are, really."

Carrie gave her a quizzical look as she attempted to make sense of the statement. "Well, it's been a while for me, too, but last time I checked, taking aspirin was perfectly permissible within the confines of a relationship."

Ash laughed. "I meant I didn't know if it would be okay for me to look for some in your medicine cabinet."

"Oh, honey." Carrie stepped in and kissed her gently on the lips. The innocence of Ash's good intentions made her heart swell. "Of course you can look for aspirin. Do you want me to get you some now?"

"No, the ice helped, but there is something else you can do for me."

"Just name it."

"Kiss me again."

"My pleasure." Carrie leaned in and pressed her lips to Ash's.

They sat back on the couch without breaking contact. Carrie couldn't believe how much she enjoyed kissing this woman. A little over a week ago she would have said that kissing was nice under the right circumstance, but she would have never believed it could be so intoxicating. Now she and Ash were making out on her couch like a couple of teenagers. She smiled when they were finally able to pull themselves apart for a second.

"I love doing that with you," Ash confessed.

"I could do it all day." Carrie grinned.

"Sounds like a good idea to me," Ash said, leaning in for another kiss.

"But," Carrie summoned all her restraint and leaned back slightly, "I have to teach at twelve thirty."

"I forgot that we had jobs," Ash said.

"You could come to the office with me," Carrie suggested, realizing that it sounded every bit like the request it was.

"I do have to get those bookshelves finished today."

Carrie blushed slightly as she said, "I don't care what excuse you use as long as I get to keep you around a little longer."

"Hmm. Well, if it means that much to you and your class isn't until twelve thirty, that leaves us an hour and a half to…" Ash reached for the belt on Carrie's robe.

"Take a shower." Carrie pushed her hand away, laughing. If Ash kept touching her like that there was no way her resolve would hold, and a big part of her didn't want it to. "You never stop, do you?"

"Do you really want me to stop?"

Carrie felt a slow smile playing at the corners of her mouth, and she shook her head. "No, but I'm afraid I'll never get anything done unless you do."

Ash appeared to be processing the dilemma for a second. "I think we can kill two birds with one stone. Come on."

She took Carrie's hand and led her back up the stairs and into the bathroom. Carrie quickly realized where this was headed and she didn't even have the will to pretend to protest. She wanted Ash's body as much as Ash obviously wanted hers. With one pull the belt's knot came undone and Ash had unfettered access to everything that lay beneath Carrie's robe. She slipped her hands under the soft terrycloth and let her hands rest on the even softer skin of Carrie's hips. Pulling her in, Ash let her mouth find its way onto Carrie's neck. Carrie gasped and threw her head back slightly as Ash nibbled on her earlobes. They'd only made love twice, but already Ash knew exactly how to drive her crazy. Carrie couldn't contain herself any longer. Needing to feel Ash's skin on her own, she dragged Ash's shirt up and off, revealing her perfect breasts and rippled abs.

Carrie groaned slightly when Ash pulled away to turn on the shower. Seconds later, they'd discarded Ash's remaining clothes and were standing beneath the steady stream of warm water. Carrie threw her head back, letting it hit her face and cascade down her body. After a few minutes, she completely surrendered to the sensations of the water, heat, and steam soaking into her body, coupled with the tender caresses of Ash's fingertips. Water pooled between them before spilling over and flooding down her belly and thighs in a sensual torrent.

"God, that feels good," Carrie practically purred.

She squeezed a dab of shampoo in her hands, reached up, and massaged the gel into Ash's short hair, spiking it up in the suds and then working it back into her scalp. The actions felt so sensual, so intimate, that she could barely control her breathing. Watching Ash standing naked under the cascading water was the most erotic thing she'd ever seen.

Ash took the bottle from the shelf, poured a liberal amount into her hands, and ran it through Carrie's long, silky curls. "Your hair is so gorgeous," she said.

Carrie had always found her hair to be boring and unruly, but when Ash reverently sank her fingers into the thick locks, working up a lather and making sure it covered every curl, she felt beautiful. "Your hands are amazing."

"Maybe we should get them together more often." Ash chuckled.

Carrie just smiled and stepped back under the water, rinsing the bubbles, letting them run down over her body. She watched as Ash's eyes once again clouded with desire. They pressed their mouths together, lips apart with playful tongues darting in and out tasting each other as well as the water that poured down over them. The liquid heat surrounded them at the same time it flowed from their bodies. Whether in the interest of time or due to their own sense of urgency, they moved quickly from aimless caresses to purposeful pressure. Ash wrapped one arm around Carrie and leaned back so she was resting against the wall, then slipped her other hand down between Carrie's legs. When her thumb found its target, Carrie released a moan and clutched her so tightly that her fingernails dug into the muscles across Ash's back. But just as Ash was about to send her over the edge Carrie felt her own caresses reach their goal, and the tables turned. Ash was now the one on the edge of climax. Carrie thought they were both sure to tumble to the ground as she felt her knees go weak and Ash's body started to shudder in her arms. But they somehow managed to cling to each other, panting under the spray of the shower, trying to catch their breath. After rinsing the remainder of the soap suds from their hair and bodies, they toweled off in a daze. When they were both dried off, it was Ash who finally said, "Now that's what I call multitasking."

CHAPTER SEVENTEEN

The process of finishing the bookcases was relatively mindless, but Ash tried to give it her full attention. She wanted the end result to be flawless. She had to open the windows to let the fumes air out of the office, and when she did she couldn't help but smile at the memory of the window that had served as a catalyst for her and Carrie's first kiss. She couldn't help but think that she'd be forever grateful for the small lock that had held it in place only a week earlier.

A week, Ash thought in amazement. She sat back in Carrie's desk chair and rubbed her forehead. She hadn't really let herself think about the complete transformation she'd undergone in such a short amount of time. The total turnaround she had gone through was enough to make anyone dizzy. Shreds of doubt began to creep into the back of her mind. What did this mean for her future?

She tried to look ahead. The first thing that entered her mind was the prospect of making love to Carrie again. Ash smiled. That was something she could see herself enjoying for the rest of her life. Realistically, though, as much as they'd both like to, they wouldn't be able to have sex every waking minute for all of eternity. What happened in between those passionate moments when their bodies collided? She didn't know what kind of music

Carrie liked, or what foods she hated. Ash didn't know anything about Carrie's family or upbringing.

She tried to think of everything she knew about Carrie. She knew she was active in the community, that she liked to read, and that she bit her nails when she was nervous. Surely there was more than that.

She thought of the conversations they'd had over the past week. Most of them had centered on Tess. Ash considered the connection. Tess was now a part of her life, and there was no denying she would remain important to Carrie, but was that enough to live on? They had also talked about their jobs. Teaching and women's studies were obviously central to who Carrie was. She seemed set on making women's voices heard at the university. Could Ash share in that?

Ash had always supported women's rights and had never conformed to society's expectations of what a woman should be, but beyond that she was at a loss. She couldn't even begin to imagine what " normative personhood" was. Would Carrie want to talk to her about things like that? Would she think less of Ash for not being able to?

She was jarred from her thoughts by a knock at the door. She stood up and walked over to answer it, shaking her head slightly in an attempt to clear it, but when she opened the door she found herself standing face-to-face with Rita.

Ash had to confess that Rita looked good. She was wearing tight black pants and a v-neck sweater that dipped just low enough to make a person look twice. She flashed a broad smile that made Ash nervous.

"Can I come in?" Rita asked.

"Uh, Carrie, um, I mean Dr. Fletcher isn't here right now."

Rita laughed. "No, I didn't think she was."

"She'll be back in about ten minutes, though," Ash continued. "You could come back then."

"If you don't mind, I'll just wait here." Rita slipped past Ash and into the office.

"Actually," Ash tried not to let her discomfort show, but the last thing she wanted was for Carrie to walk in and find her and Rita alone together in the office, "I don't know if that's a good idea."

"Just relax," Rita replied, placing her hand lightly on Ash's shoulder.

Ash started to pull away, but then she stopped. She felt Rita touching her; she could see Rita standing in front of her. She looked good, she felt good, she was practically throwing herself at Ash, but something was missing. Ash was not the least bit turned on. There was no spark, no fire, nothing. Sure, she could tell that Rita was attractive; she knew the feel of her touch wasn't unpleasant, but the temptation was gone. Everything about the woman standing in front of her fell short when viewed in comparison to what she saw, felt, and shared with Carrie.

Ash smiled. "Rita, I'm sorry, but…"

"I know," Rita sighed.

"You know?"

"It's pretty obvious that you're in love with Dr. Fletcher." She dropped her hand from Ash's shoulder.

"Yes, I am." Ash reached out and took Rita's hand. "It doesn't mean that you weren't… You're a wonderful woman, it's just that I love her. Do you understand what I'm trying to say?"

Rita gave her a slight smile. "Yes, but can you do me a favor?"

"What?" Ash asked.

"Can you not tell Dr. Fletcher about this? She's the best teacher I've got, and I don't want things to get awkward."

Ash laughed. "I think that'll be okay."

"Thanks." Rita leaned in and gave Ash a big hug.

Ash hugged her in return without thinking twice now that

the temptation was gone. However, when she heard the hinges of the office door squeak slightly she jumped back just as Carrie walked into the room. Ash immediately realized that from where Carrie was standing, the reaction made both her and Rita look guilty. She immediately searched Carrie's eyes and saw they were filled with shock and then hurt. Ash felt her heart breaking inside.

"Carrie," she said, desperate to clear up the situation. "Rita just stopped by to talk to you, and we had a little heart-to-heart."

"I can see that," Carrie replied tensely.

"I hope you don't mind, but I told her I've fallen hopelessly in love with you."

"I'm sure you did." Carrie tried to force a smile. "What was it that you needed, Rita?"

"I was working on the Butler assignment and I have the paper outline, but I just wanted to know if there was one area you wanted us to focus on more than the others."

Carrie nodded. "Absolutely. I want to see that you understand the theory, so I suggest you focus on how Butler sees normative gender binaries as restricting individuals' self-expression as well as how we are all affected by the way our discourse, or lack of discourse, on the social construction of gender impinges on our sense of identity."

"Okay," Rita responded as if taking a mental inventory of the things Carrie had just listed.

Ash, on the other hand, just leaned back against the wall, listening to the exchange, barely comprehending it. The words could have been spoken in a foreign language. She wasn't surprised that Carrie had a better grasp on complex ideas and a more extensive vocabulary that she did; that was to be expected, given their different professions. What worried her was how nonchalantly Carrie rattled off the terms and the ease with which Rita accepted them. From where Ash was sitting, the conversation seemed natural, like both women were used to hearing and using words like "discourse" and "normative" on a regular basis.

Maybe she had been right earlier. Maybe communicating with Carrie would take more than Ash was capable of giving.

"Is that all you wanted to know?" Carrie asked, her voice still tight.

"Yes. Thank you." Rita took her cue and started for the door. "I'll see you in class Monday."

"See you then." Carrie closed the door behind Rita. Avoiding Ash's outstretched hand, she said, "We need to talk."

"Carrie," Ash started, "I know that may have looked bad, but it's not what you think."

"Oh? Well, I think you've slept with one of my students. Am I wrong about that?"

"No, you're right about that, but—"

"Recently?"

"Yes." Ash rubbed her forehead. This was not going well.

"Tell me this, then, how many women have you slept with in, oh, let's say the past two weeks?"

"Carrie—"

"No," Carrie interrupted. "I think I deserve an honest answer. I'm not asking you to calculate a lifetime number, just in the time we've known each other, how many?"

"Counting you?"

She shrugged her shoulders. "Sure."

"Three." Ash hung her head.

"Three." Carrie sighed. "I've only slept with three people my entire life."

"Carrie, I wish I could take it all back, but I can't," Ash whispered.

"You and Mary were lovers, weren't you?" Carrie said with only the slightest hint of a question in her voice.

"What?" Ash asked, turning to face her.

"You and Mary," Carrie said, still biting her nail. "You two were lovers."

"A long time ago," Ash answered, shuffling her feet, uncomfortable with the topic.

"What happened?" Carrie asked softly.

Ash took a deep breath. "We were young and I was immature. She waited for me as long as she could, but I just never became the person she thought I could be."

"Because she wanted you to be someone you couldn't be?"

"No." Ash shook her head. "It wasn't that I couldn't, so much as that I wouldn't. I made a lot of mistakes, a lot of choices I'm starting to regret, but you have to believe me, that's over now. I wasn't coming on to Rita, I was saying good-bye. And not just to her, to that whole way of life. Please tell me you get that."

"I believe you, Ash. I really do, but that's a big transformation to have over a short period of time."

"I know, but that doesn't make it any less real. There will always be other women in my past, but I promise you that you are the only one I want to be with now. I'm sorry you have to live with that. If I could erase all the others I would, but I just can't do that."

"I know you can't, and I wouldn't want you to." Carrie sat down and quietly continued, "Your past is a part of you. It's gotten you where you are today."

"So you understand?" Ash asked hopefully.

"I understand." Carrie weighed her words carefully. "But I just don't know how I'm going to be able to relate to you."

"What do you mean?" Ash could hear her heart beating in her ears.

"I mean we're so different. Our pasts are so different. How am I supposed to take it when I walk in and catch another woman in your arms, one that I know you've slept with, one of my students, no less?" Carrie paused. "I don't understand how you've lived like that, and I'm beginning to think that I really don't know you at all."

"You don't know me?" Ash tried not to sound too incredulous. "Carrie, I think it's the other way around."

"Ash, I'm just being honest with you."

"Honest? You want honest. I'm not very complex. What you see is what you get. I work with my hands, I set my own hours, I like sports, and I have absolutely no idea what you were talking about with Rita."

"Where is this coming from?"

"I've been with a lot of women, but that's over. That's old news, but you speak a language I can't even begin to understand. You have conversations about the social construction of whatever. I don't even know what you mean, and that will probably be the case for as long as I live. That's not the past, that's right now and well into the future. You want to talk about not knowing someone, how about that?"

Ash was out of breath when she finished. There was a dull ache in her chest and her throat was beginning to tighten at the thought of all the fears they'd both just put into words.

"Ash, you drive a Mustang, don't you?"

"Yes."

"What year is it?"

"Sixty-four."

"And what kind of motor does it have in it?"

"The engine is a factory correct two eighty-nine V-8 with a four-barrel carburetor for two hundred ten horsepower and a four-cylinder, four-on-the-floor manual transmission," Ash rattled off.

Carrie smiled. "I have no idea what that means."

Ash raised her eyebrows at the strange direction the conversation had gone. "So what? It's just a car."

"And Judith Butler is just my job."

Ash shook her head. "It's more important to you than that."

"It's important, yes. I like what I do for a living, but so do you. Your work is an important part of you, too."

"But how do we know if it's going to be a problem in our relationship? How do I know you aren't going to resent me for not being able to talk about feminist theory?"

"How do I know you aren't going to resent me for tying you

down?" Carrie asked quickly. "There will always be women like Rita throwing themselves at you."

Ash moved over and sat next to Carrie. "No woman could ever make me resent you. You mean more to me than all the other women combined."

Carrie took her hand. "And you mean more to me than all of the feminist theorists in the world ever could."

"I love you," Ash said, drawing Carrie into her arms.

"I love you, too."

Ash was about to lean in for a kiss when she stopped. "Was it too early for me to say I love you? I mean, don't people usually wait longer than a couple of weeks for that?"

"Did you mean it?" Carrie asked

"Of course, but is that how it's supposed to go?"

"I meant it, too, and I think that it's okay to say it whenever you feel it. If there's some official timeline, I certainly don't know about it."

Ash was starting to feel a little better. "I'm so new at all this relationship stuff; I don't know what's a minor detail and what could lead to a real problem."

"I don't know, either. I'm not exactly a relationship guru. If I were, I probably would have been snatched off the market a long time ago." Carrie laughed.

Ash smiled. "Then I guess it's good that you're not, but with neither of us knowing what to do, how will we ever make this work?"

"We'll just have to learn together."

Ash thought about that for a moment. "I'm not always a very fast learner."

Carrie laughed again. "Believe it or not, neither am I, but I'm willing to try new things if you are."

"Hmm." Ash cocked an eyebrow. "I can think of a few new things I'd like to try with you right now."

"Does one of those things happen to be making love in my office?" Carried asked with a sly smile.

"Why yes, I do believe it does."

As she felt Carrie's hands run under her shirt and up her back, Ash thought that while she still felt pretty unsure about how to be in a relationship, she was certainly looking forward to learning.

EPILOGUE

Ash checked her reflection as she passed the mirror. She barely recognized herself in the rented tuxedo she was wearing. She took a second to run a hand through her hair, making sure it lay flat, and then tried to straighten her bow tie before turning to Tess.

"Well?" she asked, turning slowly so the girl could get a good look.

"What are you worried about? You look great. Carrie could barely keep her hands off you at dinner tonight." Tess laughed. "Now can we get back out there?"

"Hang on a minute." Ash turned back to the mirror. "I've never worn one of these things before. I want to make sure the tie is right before I go back out."

"God, you are so whipped," Tess muttered, stepping up and tugging the bow tie back into place.

Ash spun around. "*I'm* whipped? At least I picked out my own tux. I didn't need my girlfriend to tell me what to wear."

She alluded to the white tuxedo Tess was wearing. Tess, or rather her date, had opted for a traditional tie that tucked into a black vest. Tess had cut her hair to shoulder length, but it was still sun-streaked blond, which complemented the color of the tux.

Tess rolled her eyes. "No, you just needed her to tell you *how* to wear it."

Ash frowned and looked back at the mirror. She had to admit that Tess had her there. She would have never been able to get into the tuxedo without Carrie's help.

"No comeback?"

Ash thought for a moment. "Did you have to go shopping with Michelle to pick out her dress?"

Tess cringed. "Yes, it took her, like, seven hours."

"Well, there you have it. I stayed home and worked on the Mustang while Carrie and Mary went shopping."

"Oh well, I'd rather have spent seven hours at the mall than been in the doghouse for a week."

"I guess you're right. Do you think we are just learning to pick our battles more wisely?"

Tess shrugged. "Either that or we are both completely whipped."

"I never though I'd say this." Ash paused. "But I think I'm okay with that."

Tess nodded. "Me, too."

Ash smiled and gave Tess's white tuxedo jacket a short tug so it hugged her shoulders snugly. "All right, let's get back to our dates."

When they entered the main room of the youth center, Ash thought again how different it all felt from the first time she'd been there over six months ago. The beanbags and video games had been pushed aside for the evening to leave room for a makeshift dance floor. The walls were covered in decorations, balloons, and streamers. The lights were turned low and Michael was manning a stereo system that kept music pumping through the room. Everywhere Ash looked, there were teenagers and chaperones dressed to the nines.

The alternative prom, as the center referred to it, was the only chance most of the teens would have to take a date of their choice to a formal dance, and they were making the most of the evening.

Ash got lost in her thoughts as she watched Tess and Michelle dance in that awkward adolescent way, hands on waists while they swayed to the music. She never ceased to be amazed by the person Tess was becoming. Since she'd been living with Betty, she was happier and more easygoing. And while she still had a knack for wit and sarcasm, she was much more good-natured about how she used it. She was even having dinner with her mother once a week. They still had a long way to go, but Ash thought they might find some peace with each other down the road.

Her reflections were interrupted when a flash bulb went off a few feet from her and Betty Ryan advanced into view waving a camera. The older woman had chosen a sleek pantsuit with a sequined jacket for the prom. Ash thought it looked very mother-of-the-bride.

"It's not often I get to see you in a monkey suit." Betty laughed. "I just couldn't resist one more picture."

"Betty, if it makes you that happy, then you can take all the pictures you want."

"You know what would really make me happy?"

"Just name it."

"A spin around the dance floor."

Ash bowed. "It would be my pleasure." She took one of Betty's hands in her own and slipped the other arm lightly around her waist. She hadn't danced like that since, well, probably ever, but she tried to do her best to keep up with Betty, who must have had some ballroom training at one point.

"So, are you enjoying your first prom?" Betty asked in what Ash took as an attempt to distract her from the fact that Betty was now leading.

"Actually, I am."

"Don't sound so surprised. We all know that underneath that cool exterior, you're just a big old softie."

"There goes my reputation," Ash joked.

"Oh, honey, your reputation flew out the window the minute Carrie came downstairs wearing that dress tonight."

Ash blushed at the memory of how her knees had gone weak at the sight of Carrie's bare shoulders covered only by spaghetti straps that flowed into a snug-fitting chocolate-colored bodice before flaring out into a skirt so long it nearly touched the ground.

Betty laughed. "You've still got it bad for her, and everyone can see it."

Ash couldn't disagree with that. She was every bit as taken with Carrie as she had been the first night they'd met in the very room where she was now dancing.

When the song ended, she gave Betty another bow. "Thank you for that dance, madam." She affected a regal air.

Betty gave her a playful shove and shook her head. "Once a scoundrel, always a scoundrel."

Ash was just about to walk Betty off the dance floor when she felt a hand on her shoulder.

"Hey, good-looking, got a spot on your dance card for an old friend?"

"Always." Ash smiled, slipping her arm around Mary's waist. She was wearing a sleeveless, ankle-length charcoal dress with a shawl draped over her shoulders.

"Who would have thought ten years ago that we'd be dancing together at a prom?" Ash asked with a little laugh.

Mary just gave her a squeeze. "I think I would have. You're as full of surprises now as you were then."

"I find that hard to believe."

"Ash, you've changed more in the past six months than you have the entire time I've known you."

Ash thought about that for a second. "And what do you think of the new me? Do you like her as much as you did the one you met a decade ago?"

Mary smiled. "I can honestly say that I like you even more."

They danced in contented silence until the song faded to a close.

Mary gave Ash a big hug. "I'd tell you to save me another dance, but it looks like you're spoken for."

When Ash turned to see who Mary was looking at, her eyes met Carrie's and her heart skipped a beat. She had resigned herself to the fact that she'd never get used to seeing those amazing eyes searching her own. The space between them seemed to close automatically when the next song started. Ash felt the rise and fall of Carrie's chest under the satin of her dress with each breath she took.

"You feel amazing," she whispered.

"You, too." Carrie rested her head softly on Ash's shoulder. "I love that tux on you."

"Yeah? Well, I don't have to return it until noon tomorrow. I'll wear it all night if you want me to."

"Hmm, that does sound tempting, but I think I'll have to take it off you when we get home." Carrie paused. "Maybe we'll just leave the bow tie on, though."

Ash laughed. "You can take off or leave on whatever you want about this tux, but you look too good in that dress. I don't know how much longer I can take it."

Carrie gave her a sly smile. "And what do you plan on doing about that?"

"You'll just have to wait and see." Ash kissed her lightly on the lips.

"I'm looking forward to it." Carrie settled her head on Ash's chest and they continued to sway to the music.

Ash rested her chin gently on the top of Carrie's head and breathed deeply, inhaling the sweet smell of her shampoo, wondering if she'd ever be able to get enough of the woman in her arms.

"What are you thinking?" Carrie asked after a moment.

"How much I love you," Ash answered honestly.

"Really?"

"Yes. Why?"

"Me, too," Carrie whispered.

"So, Dr. Fletcher, I guess we're doing pretty good at this relationship business after all."

"Do you think we have it down pat yet?" Carrie's eyes met Ash's, deep blue and sparkling.

Ash shook her head. "No, I think I'm going to need a lot more practice. I'll probably have to spend the rest of my life studying you."

Carrie smiled. "Now that you mention it, I think I'll need a lot more hands-on research, too."

Pressing her lips to Carrie's, Ash murmured, "Let's start now."

As the soft familiar warmth began to spread through her body, she decided that this was going to be another enjoyable learning experience.

About the Author

Rachel Spangler has avoided getting a real job by staying in school for way too long, and she has loved (almost) every minute of it. She holds degrees in politics and government, women's studies, and English, and recently completed a master's degree in college student personnel administration from Illinois State University. Throughout her college experience, she has been actively involved with PFLAG, PRIDE, FMLA, and Safe Schools, all of which influenced various aspects of her first novel, *Learning Curve*.

Rachel and her partner, Susan, recently moved to western New York, where during the winter they make the most of the lake-effect snow on local ski slopes. In the summer, they love to travel and watch their beloved St. Louis Cardinals. Regardless of the season, Rachel always makes time for a good romance, whether she's reading it, writing it, or living it.

Books Available From Bold Strokes Books

Branded Ann by Merry Shannon. Pirate Branded Ann raids a merchant vessel to obtain a treasure map and gets more than she bargained for with the widow Violet. (978-1-60282-003-6)

American Goth by JD Glass. Trapped by an unsuspected inheritance and guided only by the guardian who holds the secret to her future, Samantha Cray fights to fulfill her destiny. (978-1-60282-002-9)

Learning Curve by Rachel Spangler. Ashton Clarke is perfectly content with her life until she meets the intriguing Professor Carrie Fletcher, who isn't looking for a relationship with anyone. (978-1-60282-001-2)

Place of Exile by Rose Beecham. Sheriff's detective Jude Devine struggles with ghosts of her past and an ex-lover who still haunts her dreams. (978-1-933110-98-1)

Fully Involved by Erin Dutton. A love that has smoldered for years ignites when two women and one little boy come together in the aftermath of tragedy. (978-1-933110-99-8)

Heart 2 Heart by Julie Cannon. Suffering from a devastating personal loss, Kyle Bain meets Lane Connor, and the chance for happiness suddenly seems possible. (978-1-60282-000-5)

Queens of Tristaine by Cate Culpepper. When a deadly plague stalks the Amazons of Tristaine, two warrior lovers must return to the place of their nightmares to find a cure. (978-1-933110-97-4)

The Crown of Valencia by Catherine Friend. Ex-lovers can really mess up your life…even, as Kate discovers, if they've traveled back to the eleventh century! (978-1-933110-96-7)

Mine by Georgia Beers. What happens when you've already given your heart and love finds you again? Courtney McAllister is about to find out. (978-1-933110-95-0)

House of Clouds by KI Thompson. A sweeping saga of an impassioned romance between a Northern spy and a Southern sympathizer, set amidst the upheaval of a nation under siege. (978-1-933110-94-3)

Winds of Fortune by Radclyffe. Provincetown local Deo Camara agrees to rehab Dr. Bonita Burgoyne's historic home, but she never said anything about mending her heart. (978-1-933110-93-6)

Focus of Desire by Kim Baldwin. Isabel Sterling is surprised when she wins a photography contest, but no more than photographer Natasha Kashnikova. Their promo tour becomes a ticket to romance. (978-1-933110-92-9)

Blind Leap by Diane and Jacob Anderson-Minshall. A Golden Gate Bridge suicide becomes suspect when a filmmaker's camera shows a different story. Yoshi Yakamota and the Blind Eye Detective Agency uncover evidence that could be worth killing for. (978-1-933110-91-2)

Wall of Silence, 2nd ed. by Gabrielle Goldsby. Life takes a dangerous turn when jaded police detective Foster Everett meets Riley Medeiros, a woman who isn't afraid to discover the truth no matter the cost. (978-1-933110-90-5)

Mistress of the Runes by Andrews & Austin. Passion ignites between two women with ties to ancient secrets, contemporary mysteries, and a shared quest for the meaning of life. (978-1-933110-89-9)

Sheridan's Fate by Gun Brooke. A dynamic, erotic romance between physiotherapist Lark Mitchell and businesswoman Sheridan Ward set in the scorching hot days and humid, steamy nights of San Antonio. (978-1-933110-88-2)

Vulture's Kiss by Justine Saracen. Archeologist Valerie Foret, heir to a terrifying task, returns in a powerful desert adventure set in Egypt and Jerusalem. (978-1-933110-87-5)

Rising Storm by JLee Meyer. The sequel to *First Instinct* takes our heroines on a dangerous journey instead of the honeymoon they'd planned. (978-1-933110-86-8)

Not Single Enough by Grace Lennox. A funny, sexy modern romance about two lonely women who bond over the unexpected and fall in love along the way. (978-1-933110-85-1)

Such a Pretty Face by Gabrielle Goldsby. A sexy, sometimes humorous, sometimes biting contemporary romance that gently exposes the damage to heart and soul when we fail to look beneath the surface for what truly matters. (978-1-933110-84-4)

Second Season by Ali Vali. A romance set in New Orleans amidst betrayal, Hurricane Katrina, and the new beginnings hardship and heartbreak sometimes make possible. (978-1-933110-83-7)

Hearts Aflame by Ronica Black. A poignant, erotic romance between a hard-driving businesswoman and a solitary vet. Packed with adventure and set in the harsh beauty of the Arizona countryside. (978-1-933110-82-0)

Red Light by JD Glass. Tori forges her path as an EMT in the New York City 911 system while discovering what matters most to herself and the woman she loves. (978-1-933110-81-3)

Honor Under Siege by Radclyffe. Secret Service agent Cameron Roberts struggles to protect her lover while searching for a traitor who just may be another woman with a claim on her heart. (978-1-933110-80-6)

Dark Valentine by Jennifer Fulton. Danger and desire fuel a high-stakes cat-and-mouse game when an attorney and an endangered witness team up to thwart a killer. (978-1-933110-79-0)

Sequestered Hearts by Erin Dutton. A popular artist suddenly goes into seclusion, a reluctant reporter wants to know why, and a heart locked away yearns to be set free. (978-1-933110-78-3)

Erotic Interludes 5: Road Games, ed. by Radclyffe and Stacia Seaman. Adventure, "sport," and sex on the road—hot stories of travel adventures and games of seduction. (978-1-933110-77-6)

The Spanish Pearl by Catherine Friend. On a trip to Spain, Kate Vincent is accidentally transported back in time—an epic saga spiced with humor, lust, and danger. (978-1-933110-76-9)

Lady Knight by L-J Baker. Loyalty and honor clash with love and ambition in a medieval world of magic when female knight Riannon meets Lady Eleanor. (978-1-933110-75-2)

Dark Dreamer by Jennifer Fulton. Best-selling horror author Rowe Devlin falls under the spell of psychic Phoebe Temple. A Dark Vista romance. (978-1-933110-74-5)

Come and Get Me by Julie Cannon. Elliott Foster isn't used to pursuing women, but alluring attorney Lauren Collier makes her change her mind. (978-1-933110-73-8)

Blind Curves by Diane and Jacob Anderson-Minshall. Private eye Yoshi Yakamota comes to the aid of her ex-lover Velvet Erickson in the first Blind Eye mystery. (978-1-933110-72-1)

Dynasty of Rogues by Jane Fletcher. It's hate at first sight for Ranger Riki Sadiq and her new patrol corporal, Tanya Coppelli—except for their undeniable attraction. (978-1-933110-71-4)

Running With the Wind by Nell Stark. Sailing instructor Corrie Marsten has signed off on love until she meets Quinn Davies—one woman she can't ignore. (978-1-933110-70-7)

More Than Paradise by Jennifer Fulton. Two women battle danger, risk all, and find in each other an unexpected ally and an unforgettable love. (978-1-933110-69-1)

Flight Risk by Kim Baldwin. For Blayne Keller, being in the wrong place at the wrong time just might turn out to be the best thing that ever happened to her. (978-1-933110-68-4)

Rebel's Quest: Supreme Constellations Book Two by Gun Brooke. On a world torn by war, two women discover a love that defies all boundaries. (978-1-933110-67-7)

Punk and Zen by JD Glass. Angst, sex, love, rock. Trace, Candace, Francesca…Samantha. Losing control—and finding the truth within. BSB Victory Editions. (1-933110-66-X)

When Dreams Tremble by Radclyffe. Two women whose lives turned out far differently than they'd once imagined discover that sometimes the shape of the future can only be found in the past. (1-933110-64-3)

Stellium in Scorpio by Andrews & Austin. The passionate reunion of two powerful women on the glitzy Las Vegas Strip, where everything is an illusion and love is a gamble. (1-933110-65-1)